JÉRÔME FERRARI was born in Paris. [...] professor of philosophy in [...] to Corsica and then to Abu [...] to international prominence [...] for his novel *The Sermon on the* [...]

GEOFFREY STRACHAN is the [...] winning translator of Andreï Makine.

"Blackly brilliant ... the story has a doomy propulsion, with its elegant flashbacks and adumbrations, vivid, economical scene-setting, and fascinating relationships at its heart"   STEVEN POOLE, *Guardian*

"A work of alluring beauty ... Ferrari's masterful narrative, shaped by a chilling wisdom, moves and unsettles in equal, unforgettable measure"   EILEEN BATTERSBY, *Irish Times*

"Brilliantly and movingly done"   ALLAN MASSIE, *Spectator* Books of the Year

"The most powerful novel I have read this year ... A devastating story that shows how the victims of torture often become torturers themselves"   MICHAEL HOLROYD, *Guardian* Books of the Year

"A short novel more admirable than enjoyable, but one that you can't get out of your head"   *Scotsman* Books of the Year

"*Where I Left My Soul* may not be an easy read – it is an unsparing examination of how violence begets violence – but it is an important one"   LUCY POPESCU, *Independent*

"A devastating study of the effects of torture on both victims and perpetrators. Though firmly rooted in the savagery of Algerian struggle for independence, the novel has modern echoes that makes it uncomfortable and illuminating"

ÁNGEL GURRÍA QUINTANA, *Financial Times* Books of the Year

JÉRÔME FERRARI

WHERE I LEFT MY SOUL

Translated from the French by
Geoffrey Strachan

MACLEHOSE PRESS
QUERCUS · LONDON

First published in the French language as *Où j'ai laissé mon âme*
by Actes Sud, Arles, 2010
First published in Great Britain in 2012 by MacLehose Press
This paperback edition published in 2013 by

MacLehose Press
an imprint of Quercus
55 Baker Street
7th Floor, South Block
London W1U 8EW

A CIP catalogue record for this book is available
from the British Library.

(MMP) 978 0 85738 909 1
(Ebook) 978 0 85705 132 5

10 9 8 7 6 5 4 3 2 1

Designed and typeset in Albertina by Libanus Press, Marlborough
Printed and bound in Great Britain by Clays Ltd, St Ives plc

for Jean-Yves Templon

TRANSLATOR'S NOTE

A number of people and organizations referred to in the original French text of Jérôme Ferrari's novel relate to the period of rebellion and war in French Algeria between 1954 and 1962 which led to Algerian independence. The F.L.N. (*Front de Libération Nationale*) was the independence movement and the A.L.N. (*Armée de Libération Nationale*) was its military wing. The revolutionary committee divided the country into six autonomous zones or *Wilayas*. Kabylia is the region of Algeria on whose coastline Algiers is situated: it has a distinct landscape and culture, the Kabylian Berber people have lived there over many centuries. The French settlers in Algeria (who left for metropolitan France after independence) were known as *pieds noirs*. The *harkis* were Algerian Muslims fighting on the French side. Général Raoul Salan was Commander-in-Chief of the French army in Algeria from 1956 until he retired in 1960. An opponent of Algerian independence, Salan was one of the generals who led an attempted coup against the French government in 1961 and launched the O.A.S. (*Organisation Armée Secrète*), using underground techniques of terrorism. Général Jacques de Bollardière, who had fought at El Alamein and in the *maquis*, and who was sent to Algeria in 1956, was shocked by the attitudes of the French army and requested posting back to France. In March 1957, a letter from him was published in *L'Express* voicing his criticisms and he was sentenced to sixty days of "fortress arrest" for this breach of discipline.

The military ranks of *caporal, sergent, adjudant-chef, sous-lieutenant, lieutenant, capitaine, commandant, lieutenant-colonel, colonel* and *général,* which I have left in French in the text, are approximately equivalent to the British military ranks of corporal, sergeant, warrant officer, second lieutenant, lieutenant, captain, major, lieutenant colonel, colonel and general.

I am indebted to a number of people, including the author, for assistance and advice in the preparation of this translation. My thanks are due, in particular, to June Elks, Ben Faccini, Scott Grant, Don Hill, Russell Ingham, Pierre Sciama, Simon Strachan and Susan Strachan, as well as Christopher MacLehose, who commissioned it.

G.S.

AUTHOR'S PREFACE

Many of them began their careers by fighting against the Nazis in 1943 or 1944, in the service of a cause about which it was impossible to have doubts. At the end of the war they remained in the Army. They were not to know that they would have almost twenty more years of fighting to do, throughout the slow and bloody death agony of the French colonial Empire. They were young officers, carried along by the wind of history, but, without their being aware of it, the wind changed and began to blow against them.

Following the victory of 1945 all they experienced was an uninterrupted series of defeats; in November 1954, some months after the disaster of Dien Bien Phu, when the Viet Minh had only just released those of them who survived the re-education camps, another war was beginning, which ended eight years later – in spite of electric-shock torture, waterboarding and summary executions – with Algerian independence.

The Algerian War opened a grievous wound in French history which has palpably not healed to this day. But it was not French wounds, nor even history, that interested me; I was only interested in the trajectory these officers followed, as a paradigm of the way in which man, as he plunges into his own inner darkness, loses his soul. I wanted to capture all that is tragic, incomprehensible and appallingly banal about this trajectory. To capture the moment when we open our eyes in horror at the mirror reflecting back at us the very image of everything we have sought to fight against.

And I fear that what Algeria has given to humanity is only one opportunity, among many others, for it to open its eyes in horror at itself.

J. F.

"He is saying that there is no peace for him by moonlight and that his duty is a hard one. He says it always, whether he is asleep or awake, and he always sees the same thing: a path of moonlight. He longs to walk along it and talk to his prisoner, Ha-Notsri, because he claims he had more to say to him on that distant fourteenth day of Nisan. But he never succeeds in reaching that path and no-one ever comes near him."

Mikhail Bulgakov, *The Master and Margarita*
Translated by Michael Glenny

I remember you, mon capitaine, I remember you clearly, and I can still picture distinctly the dark confusion and despair that filled your eyes when I told you he had hanged himself. It was a cold spring morning, mon capitaine, it was so long ago and yet for a brief moment, there in front of me I caught a glimpse of the old man you have finally become. You asked me how we could possibly have left such an important prisoner as Tahar unguarded, several times you repeated, how could you possibly? as if it were essential for you to grasp the inconceivable negligence we had been guilty of – but what answer could I give? So I remained silent, I smiled at you and at length you understood and I saw the night fall upon you, you crumpled behind your desk, all the years you had left to live coursed through your veins, they streamed from your heart and submerged you and suddenly in front of me there was an old man on the brink of death, or perhaps a little child, an orphan, abandoned beside a long desert road. You levelled your eyes filled with darkness upon me and I felt the chill breath of your impotent hatred, mon capitaine, you made no reproach, your lips tightened to hold in check the caustic torrent of words you had no right to utter and your body trembled because none of the surges of outrage that shook it could be allowed to run its course, naivety and hope are no excuse, mon capitaine, and you knew very well that you could no more be absolved of his death than I could. You lowered your eyes, I clearly remember, and muttered, you took him from me, Andreani, you took him from me, in a broken voice, and I was ashamed for you, no longer strong enough to conceal the obscenity of your distress. When you had got a grip on yourself you made a gesture without looking at me, the gesture that is used to dismiss servants and dogs, and you lost patience because I took the time to salute you, you said, just fuck off, lieutenant! but I completed my salute and punctiliously performed a regulation right turn before leaving because some things are more important than your qualms. I was glad to get out into the street, I must admit, mon capitaine, and to escape from the repellent spectacle of your agonizing and all your hopeless wrestling with yourself. I inhaled a breath of fresh air and thought perhaps I should recommend the general staff to relieve you of your duties, that I had an obligation to do so, but I quickly abandoned this idea, mon capitaine, for loyalty is the only virtue. And yet I had been so happy to meet up with you again, you know, and I still hope that you, too, at least for a while, had been happy to do so. We had lived through so many difficult times together. But no-one knows what secret law governs our souls and it quickly became clear that you had grown apart from me and we could no longer understand one another. When I agreed to take command of that special section and installed myself with my men in the villa at Saint-Eugène you became openly hostile, I remember it clearly. I could not understand it and was hurt by it, I can tell you now, our missions were not so different that you were entitled to heap your hatred and scorn upon me, we were soldiers, mon capitaine, and it was not for us to choose how to fight, I, too, should have preferred to do it differently, you know, I too, should have preferred the bloody turmoil of battle to the appalling monotony of this hunt for intelligence, but we were not given any choice. Still today I ask myself by what aberration you could have convinced yourself that your actions were better than mine. You, too, sought and obtained intelligence and there was only ever one method for obtaining this, mon capitaine, you know very well, only one, and the hideous simplicity of this method could not in any way be compensated for by your scruples, your ludicrous posturings, your sanctimoniousness and remorse, which achieved nothing, except to make a laughing stock of you and all of us along with you. When I was ordered to come and take charge of Tahar at your command post at El-Biar, I cherished a moment of hope that your delight at having captured one of the leaders of the A.L.N. might perhaps have made you more friendly, but you did not speak to me, you had Tahar taken from his cell and gave him the full military compliments, he was led to me past a file of French soldiers who presented arms to him, him, that terrorist, that son of a whore, on your orders, while I had to submit to this shame without saying a word. Oh, mon capitaine, what was the point of such a masquerade, and what were you hoping for? Was it the gratitude of this man with whom you had become infatuated to the extent of breaking down at the news of his death? But he never spoke of you, you know, not a word; he never said, Capitaine Degorce is an admirable man, or anything of the kind and I am certain that at no time, at no time, do you understand, mon capitaine, did you occupy the smallest place in his thoughts. Tahar was a hard man who was not given to your type of sentimentality, I regret having to tell you this, and, unlike you, he knew very well that he was going to die, he had no expectation of some happy outcome along the lines of those you must surely have been dreaming of in your puerile overexcitement and blindness, puerile and inexcusable, mon capitaine, you could not be unaware of what the villa at Saint-Eugène was, you could not be unaware that no-one left it alive, for it was not a villa, it was a door open onto the abyss, a gash in the canvas of the world through which people toppled into nothingness – I have seen so many men die, mon capitaine, and they all knew they would never be seen again, no-one would kiss them on the brow while reciting the Shahadah, no loving hand would piously wash their bodies or bless them before consigning them to the earth, all they had was me, and at that moment I was closer to them than their own mothers, yes, I was their mother and their guide and I escorted them into the limbo of oblivion, to the shores of a nameless river, to a silence so complete that prayers and promises of salvation could not disturb it. In one sense Tahar was lucky that you had shown him to the press, we had to hand over his body, but if it had been up to me, mon capitaine, I should have dissolved him in quicklime too, I should have buried him in the depths of the bay, I should have scattered him to the desert winds, I should have erased him from people's memories. I should have caused him never to have existed. Tahar knew it, he knew what it is to have an enemy. But you never grasped any of this, mon capitaine, we do justice to our enemy not with our compassion or our respect, for which he has no use, but with our hatred, our cruelty – and our joy. You may perhaps remember that little student from a seminary, a conscript some stupid pen-pusher who knew nothing about our mission had assigned to me as assistant, a religious zealot, like you, afflicted with a sensitive soul, but a genuinely sensitive one, very much more innocent and honest than yours. When he arrived he was relieved because he thought he would not have to dirty his hands and he was, in a manner of speaking, safe from sin. He reported to me and I almost dismissed him. He gazed out of the windows of the villa at the sea and the laurels in the garden and could not help smiling, I think he had never seen so much light and space, he felt more alive than he had ever been, liberated from damp dawns on his knees on the chilly stone floor of some murky chapel, liberated from shameful whisperings in the dim light of a musty confessional, and I kept him on, after all it was not my place to make decisions about which lesson each of us was to take, whatever the cost, nor who was to be excused, mon capitaine, for when it comes down to it every one of us has had to pay attention, right to the end, to the same timeless and brutal lesson and nobody asked us whether we were willing to hear it, so I told the little seminarist that he would have to take notes when suspects were being interrogated, I dictated a few sentences to him, his handwriting was neat, energetic and elegant and I let him find a billet. He came back to see me, he was shattered, he said to me, please sir, it's impossible, the walls in the barrack room are covered in pornographic photographs and he asked me to have them taken down, he was stammering, I told him I did not deal with matters of this kind and that he must simply look away, and he left the room, but later I found him sitting on the edge of his bed beside his open kitbag, staring at the photographs, his mouth agape, his hands clasping an appalling black wooden crucifix and he looked so vulnerable, mon capitaine, almost as much as you did when I told you Tahar had hanged himself, but in his case, I could understand it, all he had known was the looming shade of the Virgin, swathed in her long blue mantle, the pure tears of Mary Magdalene and the celestial ecstasies of Saint Teresa of Avila, and now he could not take his eyes off these women spreading their legs before him with their brutish tufts, their glistening genitalia, open, as if cut with knives, and he felt the fires of hell consuming the marrow of his bones, as he clutched the body of Our Lord, but nothing could make him look away. The next day, I made him witness his first interrogation, he sat in a corner of the room, his notebook on his knees, he said nothing when we suspended the Arab from the ceiling, as if, since his arrival, he could do nothing but open his eyes wide, simmer and remain silent, and I was grateful to him, mon capitaine, for having understood so quickly that there was nothing to be said. I applied the electrodes to the ear and penis. He watched the naked body rear and tense and the huge mouth, distorted with shouting, he watched the water flowing and soaking the rag fastened to the face of the Arab whose flayed heels struck the ground staining the wet cement with blood. When we removed the damp rag and the Arab, after panting like an animal, said he would talk, my little seminarist was still staring and I had to remind him that he must take notes now. Every day he endured the deadly tedium of that ceremony over which you and I, mon capitaine, so often presided, the repetition of the same unchanging routines that assembled us around the ugliness of naked bodies and, for as long as he remained with me, he carried out his duties without ever complaining. He found a place on the wall for his crucifix, in amongst the photographs, he followed the men into Si Messaoud's brothel in the High Casbah and accepted being completely changed for ever, accepted becoming the man he had become in spite of himself, unresisting, without boasting, but this was something you never accepted, mon capitaine, you never rose to the challenge of your destiny, all you could ever do was to make desperate efforts to hurl far away from yourself the being you were in the process of becoming and, of course, you did become it all the same. Everything that lies beyond the delicate ebb and flow of your own soul is a matter of indifference to you, and you only care about what might sully the graven image you have erected to yourself, and at which you worship. So there you are, Capitaine André Degorce, resistance fighter, deported at the age of nineteen, survivor of the battle of Dien Bien Phu and the camps of the Viet Minh. History awarded you an official victim's diploma once and for all and you have hung on to it desperately, unable to do anything other than wear yourself out vainly seeking to formulate subtle distinctions, utterly meaningless, of course, as to what is clean and what is dirty, what is worthy of you and what is not, with what degree of delicacy one should treat one's enemies, and you must have regretted that no manual of etiquette exists which might have calmed your debutante's anxieties. But you are incapable of love and compassion, apart from the theoretical compassion of parish priests, that abstract love for a fellow human being who does not exist. When the killers sent by Tahar wiped out Si Messaoud's brothel, mon capitaine, I went to the site with my section, remember, you and I ran into one another there, and I had all the men in the nearby houses who claimed to have heard nothing arrested. Si Messaoud's head had been placed on a stone bench in the entrance hall. We found the girls piled up in the patio, their guts strewn over the marble paving stones. The seminarist did not vomit. He wept, mon capitaine, he wept for a long time over the girls' bodies, recalling the warmth and comfort, recalling the kisses, he wept and could not stop, but the following night, when the neighbours were being interrogated, he was no longer weeping, he hit them in the small of the back with a length of hosepipe one after the other, he turned the handle of the generator and, even if we obtained nothing that night, it was only thus, much more than with his tears, that he showed the reality of his compassion. That is what compassion can do, but it is, of course, something you are absolutely incapable of understanding, disembowelled prostitutes don't deserve the favour of your notice, they don't merit the pain inflicted on those men who blocked their ears and let them die, nor that on those who massacred them, starting with Tahar, whose bogus moralistic posturing you admired to the extent of according him the full military compliments, before my eyes, mon capitaine, before my very eyes, without a thought for the terror of the whores, without a thought for the young people at the Milk Bar, blown to pieces by the bomb Tahar sent them to pay them back for being young and happy-go-lucky, without a thought for anything other than yourself and your amazing warrior's nobility. The young people who died at the Milk Bar are long forgotten, but you have not even had to forget them, mon capitaine, you quite simply never gave them a thought. Maybe you are right, what point is there in thinking about what is bound to be forgotten? They were listening to music and drinking lemonade, and a young woman came in, a fair-skinned girl from Kabylia who set down the bag containing the bomb beside the counter, no-one turned to look at her as she left, the boys were too busy watching the girls' breasts stirring beneath the light fabric of their summer dresses, they were making utterly silly remarks, which were silenced by the explosion, they were not worth much, mon capitaine, they were very sure of themselves, bursting with arrogance and scorn, but they were our own, just as the whores were, their worth is immaterial, it was simply incumbent on us to bear witness that they had lived. It was our duty to bear witness, with the water, the electricity, the knife, with all the force of our compassion. Everything gets forgotten so quickly, mon capitaine, everything is so weightless. I went back there, you know, a few years ago, in an almost empty aircraft. No-one remembers us. At the airport the policeman stamped my passport and wished me a pleasant stay. Maybe he took me for a *pied-noir* suffering from nostalgia who wanted to revisit his childhood home before he died. But probably he didn't even ask himself any questions. The city resembles a decrepit old lady pickled in her own filth, falling apart beneath the tawdry rags of her former glory. In front of the Milk Bar the Emir Abd el-Kader holds aloft the sword of victory and the streets are named after the terrorists we killed. But don't be deceived, mon capitaine, they, too, have been forgotten, their sanctification has made them disappear for ever, more surely than silence could have done. I went and took a room at the Hôtel Saint-George, there were damp patches on the walls and ceramic tiles missing, but the air in the garden was scented with jasmine just as it was forty years ago when I used to leave the villa to drink a whisky in the winter sunlight. I took a taxi and the driver asked me what I was doing there, in the end I told him a lie, I said I was feeling homesick and before I died I wanted to see the house I had lived in as a child. He offered to take me there and I said I would wait and see. He grumbled about the water being cut off and about his job which meant he had to drive around at night and run the risk of meeting a dummy road block, this had happened to him once, he had even burned his tongue swallowing his lighted cigarette, you see, mon capitaine, the Islamists don't like smokers, that's something they have in common with your old friends in the F.L.N., their disgusting moralism, and the taxi driver laughed at how he had got away with it. I asked him to put me down at the Place des Martyrs and to wait for me there a moment. I walked past the mosque of the Jews and went up into the Casbah. Children were playing amid the refuse and rubble, a man was listening to music in a dark room and swaying backwards and forwards, his face in his hands, and I felt as if I could have walked about in this labyrinth without getting lost, just like in those days so long ago, when we used to leap from rooftop to rooftop, mon capitaine, and Tahar's men used to go to ground like rats in that maze of wells and dark arcades as they learned to fear us. But I retraced my footsteps and told the driver to do a tour of the city before taking me back to the hotel. We drove along beside the sea, to Saint-Eugène, I saw the villa, nowadays it must belong to a high-ranking officer and I'm sure the ghosts I left there do not trouble his sleep. I did my work well. We drove up towards El-Biar, past a building from which the music for a wedding was spilling out, and the taxi driver joined in the song, a very old song which Belkacem, the *harki* in my section, often used to sing, I remember it clearly, oh, if my soul were in my hands, a very well known song, you must have heard it yourself, mon capitaine, I love you, Sara, let me live in your heart, you are my life, Sara. The taxi driver was singing at the top of his voice, I could die for you, Sara, and he seemed happy for me to hum along with him. Don't leave me, Sara. You've left your mark in my heart, it will never depart. At the hotel I gave him a thousand dinars and told him that, on reflection, I was not all that keen to see my childhood home again. He insisted on my taking his telephone number in case I needed it. He shook my hand. Everything is so weightless, mon capitaine, everything is so swiftly forgotten. The blood of our people and the blood we shed has all been washed away long ago by fresh blood, and that, too, will soon be washed away in turn. I read the newspapers amid the cool of the jasmine. Seventeen customs officers killed at Timimoun. Three policemen decapitated at Sétif. Between Béchar and Taghit a whole wedding procession had their throats cut in a dummy roadblock. Everything is so weightless. The bride may have been called Samia, or Rym, or Nardjess. Who remembers? Our actions lack gravity, mon capitaine, but you are too proud to accept this. Can you not see? Our actions carry no weight, they count for nothing, a race of men may once have existed who knew this, perhaps the ones who slit the wedding couple's throats still know this, but as for us, we have grown sensitive, we are no longer capable of purging ourselves of our past deeds, purely and simply, as if they were shit, and we poison ourselves, our past deeds poison us, we suffocate from denial or from self-justification and here I am in one way just like you, mon capitaine, even if this fact gives me no joy, if I had not been like you, if I had not attached exaggerated importance to my past deeds, I should not have joined the O.A.S., I should have gone home and thought about something else. But there it is, amid the general amnesia, I have total recall, I remember everything clearly. One cannot be loyal without memory, and, as I have said, I am loyal. Yes, mon capitaine, of the two of us I am the one who betrayed the Republic and yet I am the one who proved himself loyal. I am not talking about Eternal France, the integrity of the Nation, the honour of arms or of the flag, all those flimsy, ill-considered abstractions upon which you sought to build your life, I am talking about the concrete and fragile things of which we were the trustees, the howling of Si Messaoud's whores, my seminarist's tears, the foolish giggling of the girls at the Milk Bar, the song sung by the *harki*, Belkacem, whom you and your like abandoned to his death in 1962 in the name of your peculiar sense of duty, I am speaking of everything that you betrayed without the slightest qualm, and it is to this alone that I owe my loyalty, it does not matter that in the end it should all be totally forgotten. But you do not care about the world, you are sunk in bemused contemplation of the exceptional tragedy it has been your lot to live through, you are still asking yourself how it was possible for you to become a torturer and a murderer. Oh, but it is the truth, mon capitaine, there is nothing impossible about it: you are a torturer and a murderer. There is nothing you can do about it now, even if you are still unable to accept it. The past disappears and is forgotten, but nothing can undo it. No-one cares about you anymore, apart from yourself. The world no longer knows who you are and God does not exist. No-one will punish you for what you have done, no-one will grant you the redemption along with the chastisement your pride demands. Your prayers are vain. Have you learned nothing? Are you so irremediably blind? You have lived through nothing exceptional, mon capitaine, the world has always teemed with men like you, and no victim has ever had the slightest difficulty in turning himself into a torturer, given the tiniest change in circumstances. Remember this, mon capitaine, it is a brutal lesson, timeless and brutal, the world is old, it is so old, and men's memories are so short. What has been played out in your life has already been played out on similar stages an incalculable number of times, and the millennium just beginning will offer nothing new. It is no secret. Our memories are short. We disappear like generations of ants and everything has to start all over again. The world is a hopeless teacher, all it is capable of doing is repeating the same things over and over again and we are recalcitrant pupils, not until the lesson has been painfully inscribed into our own flesh do we pay attention, we look elsewhere and are noisily indignant as soon as we are brought into line. If life had not made a soldier of you, mon capitaine, if you had not been obliged to sit in the front row in class, you, too, would have been indignant, you might have sent articles of protest to your friends at *L'Humanité*, you might have held forth about the inalienable rights of every human being, about their dignity, contemplating your own elegant, unsullied white hands with admiration all the while, never dreaming for a moment that a torturer's heart beats in your breast. But life did not allow you to enjoy this luxury. You know all about the dignity of human beings, you know what men are worth, including you and me. When we got to the camp in Vietnam after the battle of Dien Bien Phu, I remember it very well, it was you who first taught me this, as you taught me so many other things. We were sitting there, exhausted and hungry, with a group of prisoners and you said to me, I know what a camp is, Horace, in a few days' time we shall not be able to count on most of our comrades, what you will see making his appearance is man and you will have to learn to defend yourself against him, man, naked man, those were your very words, I remember clearly and you were right. Have you forgotten? Have you ended up convincing yourself that you were superior to the human species? Men are not worth very much, mon capitaine. Generally speaking they are worth nothing. They cannot be singled out according to their worth. The only thing to go by is partiality. All you can do is to recognize your own people and be loyal to them. But for you that is impossible, you cannot help making judgements, your inordinate passion for making judgements is such that, not content with judging yourself, you did not hesitate for a second to dishonour yourself and all of us with you, in order to win the esteem of a man like Tahar, and even today you are ready to seek absolution from anyone who comes along, like a young lad ashamed of groping the maid. Yours is a strange pride, mon capitaine. But I ask you this – who can judge us? The God you believe created this world? The nation in whose name we have fought throughout our lives and which has shown its gratitude by relegating us to the stinking lower depths of its bad conscience? They sentenced me to death, mon capitaine, then they pardoned me and granted me amnesty and while they had the right to kill or spare me, that makes no odds, they did not have the right to condemn or pardon me, and in no case did they have the right to grant me amnesty, they have no right to judge us, we are beyond their comprehension, their blame or praise are nothing. I should so have liked you to come to realize this. We have received the world's lesson, we have attended to its timeless, brutal teaching, and we have both, you and I, been the instruments of its pitiless pedagogy. Yes, you too, mon capitaine. Every time you exposed their nakedness to the light, each time metal and flesh penetrated their bodies, each time you stopped their eyes closing, when you brought them back into consciousness by force, with each breath of air refused, with each burn, you, too, were in the business of educating all those who passed through your hands. But you were never present at their deaths and you cannot know how it was. I have seen so many men die, mon capitaine, I was closer to them than their own mothers and I can assure you that they had all learned something, something important, a truth Tahar never knew because you did not want him to receive even a little rough treatment. At night we would drive out of the city and fly over the bay, they would be silent in the back of the lorry or in the helicopter, they would not weep, they would not beg, there was neither any desire or rebellion left in them, and they toppled into the common grave without a cry, they plummeted into the sea in a long, silent fall, they were not afraid, I know because I looked into the eyes of every one of them, as was my duty, mon capitaine, death is a serious matter, but they were not afraid, we gave them a gentle death, we did that for them, they returned my gaze, they could see my face and their eyes were empty, I remember distinctly, there was no trace of hatred to be found in them, no judgement, no yearning, there was no longer anything there, apart, perhaps, from tranquillity and relief at being finally liberated, for thanks to us, mon capitaine, none of them could fail to be unaware that the body is a tomb.

27 MARCH, 1957: FIRST DAY
Genesis iv, 10

From the top of the vast organization chart that fills a whole section of the office wall Tarik Hadj Nacer, known as Tahar the Pure, seems to view the world with inordinate melancholy. At the time when this photograph was taken at a police station in Constantine, he had not yet acquired his nickname. He was simply an employee in a bank with subversive ideas and even if he was beginning to grasp that he could no longer escape his future as a warlord in a clandestine war, he may well have been resigning himself to it without enthusiasm. Two months earlier, when Capitaine André Degorce moved in, Tahar had presided there all alone, like the sovereign of an invisible kingdom, at the top of a blank organization chart, which is now almost entirely covered by dozens of names and photographs, most of them marked with a little red cross. When not one of the boxes remains empty Capitaine André Degorce will have finished his task. He knows it is only a matter of time now and he also knows that when that day arrives he will be incapable of rejoicing at his victory. All his life he has cherished dreams of victory, without ever knowing anything other than a long series of defeats, but it would never have occurred to him that on the eve of his wish finally being granted he would have to discover how cruel victory can be and that it would cost him a great deal more than all he had to give. He can no longer pray. In vain he kneels in the dim light of his bedroom, straining after fervour, as he has done since childhood, no word rises to his lips. He remains motionless in the silence, letting himself be lulled by the regular beating of his numbed heart until he finally decides to open his Bible at random and softly read out several verses that bring him no comfort. He no longer finds messages of hope in the scriptures, only the endlessly repeated expression of a terrifying threat. He can no longer receive letters from Jeanne-Marie without trembling. Every day he delays opening them for fear of learning that he has already received his punishment. He imagines that his nephew has suddenly been taken ill or his daughter has died, carried off in a few days by pneumonia, or knocked over by a car, on account of what he is doing here.

(*I know who you are. I have listened to your voice for a long time. You are a jealous God, visiting the iniquity of the fathers upon the children unto the third and fourth generation.*)

Yet again this morning he does no more than stroke the envelope with his fingertips and smell the perfume before summoning an N.C.O.

"Febvay, tell the Kabylian I'm coming to see him. Put the others with him into another cell. Take him some cigarettes. And tea. Be friendly. Tell him there will be no more questioning. I just want to come and have a talk. Call me when everything's ready."

Capitaine Degorce lights a cigarette and smokes it carefully, leaning his brow against a window pane. The sun is shining on the bay and there are no clouds over the sea, but the sky is not really blue, it is streaked with faded, yellowish trails, that give it the dull, dirty colour of the water in a pond. In this country the sky is never blue, not even in summer, especially not in summer, when the burning desert wind blurs the outlines of the city with eddies of ochre dust and a haze of glittering mist floats up from the dead waves of the Mediterranean where the red hulls of the freighters bob up and down. He remembers a holiday spent with Jeanne-Marie and the children back in Corsica in April two years before, breakfast on the terrace of a hotel in Piana, looking across to the Golfo di Porto, the incredibly clearly defined silhouette of the rocky pinnacles against the deep blue of a limpid sky and finds it hard to believe that the coastline he is looking at today is washed by the same sea, one that spreads out beneath the same sky.

He banishes the image of his daughter smiling in the autumn sunlight. He wishes that what he is about to do was already done.

"Everything's ready, mon capitaine."

*

The Kabylian is leaning against the wall. He is naked, wrapped in a dirty blanket. He rests his big green eyes upon the capitaine who sits down cross-legged, facing him.

"You look as if you're getting over it," says the capitaine, putting a hand on his shoulder.

The Kabylian represses a moan of pain and tries to shake himself free. The capitaine withdraws his hand.

"You've been very brave, you know. My men were all very

impressed. They respect you a great deal. Anyway, it's finished now. The sergent must have told you. We're not monsters. Everyone knows you won't speak. We won't go on. There would be no point. I'm full of admiration."

The capitaine lights a cigarette and offers one to the Kabylian.

"Full of admiration," he insists. "I've been through it all, you know, in 1944. I know what I'm talking about."

The Kabylian shrugs. The capitaine gives an amused little laugh.

"I see you accept my cigarettes but not my admiration. Isn't that so, Abdelkrim?"

The Kabylian gives a start.

"It's a fine name, Abdelkrim Ait Kaci. A warrior's name, a noble one. You were wrong to conceal it from us for so long. Besides, you see, you didn't gain much by it. Not everyone is as brave as you."

The capitaine leans forward.

"We don't like this work, but we're good at it," he concludes in icy tones. Then he sits upright and draws calmly on his cigarette.

(*I'm playing a part, I'm a clown playing a part in a grim farce. A farce that has to be played out to the end, with no escape or remission. Every hair on my head is counted, every lie, every shameful trick. And the performance has to continue to the very end.*)

"As I told you, Abdelkrim, we shall not question you any further. But to set our minds at rest, now that we have your name, we'll be putting a few questions to members of your family. Possibly to your young sister, who is sixteen, I believe, and has the same magnificent green eyes as you, I'm prepared to wager. My men would be really keen to question her."

Abdelkrim begins trembling. He buries his face in his hands.

"My men would also be happy to question your mother. They'll question any one at all, you know."

Abdelkrim's chest is racked with sobs and tears spill out between his fingers.

"I belong to the rebellion," Abdelkrim says through his tears.

Capitaine Degorce runs a hand through his hair in a gentle, almost fatherly, gesture.

"Ah well, as for that, I know that already. I didn't need you to tell me that, for heaven's sake. I'm not an idiot, you know. It's not enough, Abdelkrim. That's by no means enough."

(*No, it's not enough. And feeling nauseous is not enough, nor is the rotten taste in one's mouth. I must go on. On the day of Judgement you will summon the just to your right hand. Will you summon Abdelkrim? And what of me? What will you do with me? To what circle of hell will you wish to relegate me, among what kind of sinners?*)

Abdelkrim gives an address. A street in the European quarter near the Boulevard du Telemly.

"Who shall I find at this address?" the capitaine asks.

"I've no idea!"

"Perhaps your sister will know? Or your mother? She'll know, won't she?"

"No! I swear to God I've no idea! All I know is it's an address we use. Before God, I swear it," Abdelkrim yells, seizing the capitaine's jacket.

"Calm down. I believe you. I'll go and see."

But Abdelkrim cannot stop weeping and shaking.

"One last thing and I'll leave you alone. Three names. The one who recruited you and the two you recruited yourself."

Abdelkrim gives the three names. Capitaine Degorce gets up and knocks on the door to summon Sergent Febvay. Abdelkrim is still in tears.

"Sergent, don't leave him alone, please. Not for a second. I don't want him playing silly buggers with us."

The capitaine squats beside Abdelkrim.

"Your sister and mother will never hear anything from us. You have my word."

Abdelkrim weeps even more.

*

"Moreau, get a vehicle and two men. We're going to Telemly. We'll leave in twenty minutes."

Capitaine Degorce marks the photograph of Abdelkrim pinned to his organization chart with a red cross. He writes the names he has just learned in the empty spaces next to it and passes them on to the general staff. He feels empty and disorientated. He sits on his desk and lights a cigarette, stubs it out at once. He picks up the letter from Jeanne-Marie and tears open the envelope in almost a single movement. "André, my child, my love, we think about you so much . . ." He puts the letter down and passes his hand over his face with a sigh. The relief that has just flooded through him quickly disappears and he finds himself alone once more, hopelessly numbed by a weariness so absolute he feels he will never recover from it. He looks up at the organization chart. He tries to tell himself that each red cross represents a bomb that will not go off. He tries to think of all the people whose lives have been saved and who will never know. But all this remains remote and abstract and all he can manage to summon up are vague, faceless ghosts.

(*One cannot count lives saved, one can only count deaths. I'm so weary of counting deaths. There is no end to my powerlessness.*)

He was trained in the use of that supreme logical system, mathematics. Once the givens of the problem have been clearly established, each inference has been rigorously derived from the preceding inference and Capitaine Degorce is compelled to admit that this splendid deductive chain imposes itself with the authority of absolute necessity, to which human reason is obliged to yield. He has long sought a flaw, but there is no flaw. From the givens of the problem the solution follows. It is very simple and there is nothing he can do about it. He is confronted by a conclusion that he can neither reject nor accept, and even if the entirety of his intellectual faculties is as if anaesthetized by it, he must daily set in motion without delay the practical consequences which this conclusion in its turn implies. The prisoners must talk. Everyone must talk. And it is strictly impossible to distinguish in advance those who remain silent in order to withhold information from those who have nothing to tell. Only the ordeal of pain distinguishes them. If it were possible the whole city should be questioned. There is nothing Capitaine Degorce can do about it. The only thing within his power is not to go beyond what logic demands.

In January the owner and the inmates of a brothel in the High

Casbah were massacred. Perhaps because the F.L.N. had placed a ban on prostitution and alcohol within the Arab quarter, perhaps because Si Messaoud, the brothel keeper, used to give information to the army. Perhaps for both reasons. When Capitaine Degorce, together with Moreau, his company adjudant-chef, and several *harkis* arrived at the site Lieutenant Horace Andreani's men were in the middle of loading half a dozen Arabs with bruised faces into a lorry. They were surrounded by weeping women.

"How's things, André?" the lieutenant inquired.

Capitaine Degorce gave him a filthy look.

"Kindly use my rank when addressing me, lieutenant."

Andreani grinned and muttered something inaudible. The capitaine went over to the group of prisoners.

"So what have they done, these men?" he asked the *harki* in Andreani's section. The *harki* turned to the lieutenant and said nothing.

"Go ahead, Belkacem, answer the capitaine," Andreani said.

"They sleep too heavily, mon capitaine. Or else they're forgetful. Or maybe they're deaf. We'll see if we can cure them."

Belkacem went over to the prisoners and started yelling in Arabic, hitting them and kicking them. The women all began wailing together.

"Let's go," Andreani gave the command. "Good day to you, mon capitaine."

Despite the fury suffocating him, Capitaine Degorce said nothing. He had no power over Andreani and in any case he could not absolutely swear that these arbitrary arrests would not lead to something. He said nothing. He walked round the brothel, pausing for a few moments in front of the corpses.

(*An unspeakable life. An unspeakable death.*)

When he emerged an old woman took him by the hand and began addressing him rapidly through her tears.

"What's she saying?"

"She says her son has done nothing, mon capitaine," a *harki* explained. "She says he's innocent and you must bring him back. Also, she blesses you."

(*Everyone should talk. Everyone.*)

The capitaine withdrew his moistened hand and stepped aside. "Tell her there's nothing I can do."

*

"If the Kabylian is taking the piss, he won't forget it in a hurry," Adjudant-chef Moreau says.

Their vehicle has just parked on the Boulevard du Telemly. The sky has suddenly grown dark and for several minutes a fine, freezing rain has been falling. The concierge at the block of flats eyes the officers disapprovingly. She confirms that there is indeed an Arab in one of the flats, a Monsieur Sahraoui, but a very well mannered, well educated gentleman, living on the third floor, and seems outraged that he might be suspected of anything at all.

"This is what we are going to do, *madame*. You will come up with us and tell M. Sahraoui that there is some mail for him. Agreed?"

"Oh no, capitaine! I can't tell lies to this gentleman. In my

39

profession, it's a matter of trust . . ."

"You'll do what the capitaine tells you and shift your fat arse,"
cuts in Adjudant-chef Moreau. "Otherwise I swear you'll be taken
away, you and all your family. You can put on your airs and graces in
a regrouping camp. Get it?"

The concierge's jaw drops in horror and she complies without
another word.

(*Logic reigns supreme and we are the masters of the city.*)

They make their way up the staircase as silently as possible. The
muted sound of his own footsteps gives Capitaine Degorce an
uneasy feeling he cannot shake off. On the third floor Moreau indi-
cates the door to the concierge with a threatening finger. She
knocks. The capitaine cocks his revolver.

"Monsieur Sahraoui? There's some mail for you."

After a few moments the door opens. The capitaine will never
forget this moment. He has studied this face at the top of the organization chart for so long that he cannot doubt for a second that this
is indeed him, now strangely endowed with a tangible, frail body,
but at the same time it is quite impossible for this to be him, for the
man standing on the threshold has seen the gun, he has seen the
camouflage battledress and yet he continues smiling, as if all this
were simply a chance encounter with dear, long lost friends.

"Are you Tarik Hadj Nacer?" the capitaine asks and the man
replies "yes" while continuing to smile. It is an extremely gentle and
warm smile, in no way tainted with any hint of defiance or irony.

"You are Tahar?" the capitaine insists.

"Yes, capitaine. I am."

The colonel has called a press conference for 18.00 hours. Despite his pointing out that a trap had been set on the Boulevard du Telemly where Moreau had orders to arrest anyone who asked to see M. Sahraoui, Capitaine Degorce had not been able to obtain any further postponement.

"Think about it, Degorce. They'll know all about it before the journalists have finished writing their stories. It'll be a busted flush within a couple of hours, your trap. If you're going to arrest anyone it'll be now or never. Believe me."

Capitaine Degorce nodded and a few minutes later Moreau rang to report that he had just arrested a young woman, a so-called niece, who refused to give her name.

"Excellent, Moreau. Come back here with your package. But leave someone there until tomorrow morning all the same. You never know."

The colonel is delighted.

"Good work, Degorce, even though you had a hell of a stroke of luck! Hell's bells! This'll give these scum a kick in the balls. Come on, then. Let's have a look at him, your Hadj Nacer."

Tahar is sitting on a mattress, his hands tied, his eyes half closed. He looks as if calmly lost in meditation and his strange smile has still not disappeared. The colonel does his number as a magnanimous and victorious warrior and starts pacing up and down the cell, holding forth in a grandiloquent manner about the profession of arms, visibly taking pleasure in listening to the sound of his own voice, wondering aloud how he, the colonel, would have acted had he been an Arab, and conceding that he would doubtless have followed the same course, he has always known how to put himself in the shoes of his enemies, he congratulates Tahar on having caused him so many problems, he becomes intoxicated with his own words, swearing enthusiastically. Capitaine Degorce dreads meeting Tahar's eye, and looks down, overwhelmed by the weight of his shame.

(*He's an imbecile. Always has been. The man's total and utter imbecility is mind-blowing.*)

The muffled cry of a woman can be heard. The colonel pays no attention to it.

"I'll be back," Capitaine Degorce says and leaves the cell.

He goes into a hall at the end of the corridor. A very young woman lies stretched out on a table, with her wrists and ankles attached to its legs. Two *harkis* and Sergent Febvay are bending over her. Her nose is bleeding, she is naked: a handkerchief has been stuffed into her mouth. The capitaine eyes her breasts, the curve of her pale belly, the curls of her tuft, from out of which the dark and gleaming mass of an automatic pistol appears to thrust forth. For a moment it seems to him, furtively and unbearably, that she is grimacing and writhing amid the pains of a monstrous birth. In a corner of the room Adjudant-chef Moreau smokes a cigarette.

(*Logic knows no bounds. Its reign is unlimited. The Gehenna of fire.*)

"This is the bitch from Telemly," Sergent Febvay says. "We're trying to get some sense out of her."

"Remove that," says the capitaine, indicating the gun thrust into her belly. "Remove that at once."

The sergent obeys.

"Are you insane, Moreau? The press are coming and this is all you could think of doing? Get that girl dressed and send her packing."

"Do we really have to get her dressed, mon capitaine?" Febvay asks. "It's a shame for the wogs," he goes on, indicating the *harkis*. "It'd be a change for them from fucking goats."

The *harkis* start laughing. Capitaine Degorce takes a couple of steps towards the sergent and raises his hand to hit him, but restrains himself and his arm falls back loosely beside his body. He knows he should not have raised his hand and also knows that, having once raised it, he should not have lowered it. He speaks in an unrecognizable voice.

"I'll have you court-martialled, you bag of shit. Court-martialled, do you understand? I'll have you shot."

The adjudant-chef goes up to him and gently takes the capitaine by the arm.

"With respect, mon capitaine, what was all that about?"

The capitaine stands stock-still for a long moment. He finds it difficult to meet the sergent's eye. He moves towards the door with a haste he finds detestable.

"Get that girl dressed, Moreau," he says in a shaking voice. "And find the sergent an assignment where his sense of humour will be appreciated for its true worth. Anywhere, I don't give a damn. Get him out of my sight."

43

Once out in the corridor he makes a swift about turn and marches back into the room. No-one has moved. He goes straight up to Sergent Febvay and knees him in the groin. The sergent collapses almost without a sound and Degorce lands a blow with his fist on the side of his head, using all his strength. The sergent falls, his knees drawn into his chest without even essaying a gesture of self-defence. Capitaine Degorce massages his painful hand. He observes the young man moaning at his feet. At first he feels the dazzling joy of relief. And immediately after this, pity, remorse – unspeakable powerlessness.

*

The journalists have come and gone. Tahar has smiled, handcuffed, amid the crackle of flash photographs. The colonel has congratulated himself on the exceptional importance of this arrest, which, he was confident, had dealt the rebellion an almost mortal blow. The colonel indicated to the journalists that they could put questions to the prisoner. Aren't you ashamed to use women for your terrorist attacks? Do you have any feelings of remorse? Are you afraid of the guillotine? What have you to say to the families of your victims? Why do you carry on with a struggle that is already lost? Do you beg the French Republic for clemency? Tahar has listened attentively to all the questions and looked at each of the journalists with a great deal of benevolence, but has not said a word. Standing beside him, Capitaine Degorce studied the toecaps of his shoes. He was no longer even trying to shake off the grip of humiliation. He was simply waiting for the whole charade to be at an end. It occurred to him that Jeanne-Marie would see his picture in the papers next morning and would in all probability be proud of him. If she were to learn one day what he was really doing here she would be unable either to believe it or to understand it. And she would be right: in spite of all the logic in the world, it was at bottom impossible to understand and it was better for his wife to remain in permanent ignorance.

(*How could I take her in my arms? How could I embrace the children? What could I tell them?*)

When they first met in spring 1945 he was twenty and weighed five and a half stones. She was ten years older than him and a war widow. Her husband had spent months dying of boredom on the Maginot line. He used to write that he missed her and was eager to fight and occasionally ventured upon rather daring references to chilly nights spent without her. In his last letter he wrote again that he would be ready for the Germans when they came and would love her all his life. He never had to fight. After the German offensive he fled south with all the surviving men in his battery, desperate as they were and almost without ammunition. He must have hoped he could reach Toulon or Marseille, somewhere he could find a boat to take him home to her in Corsica. But one evening when he and his comrades were resting in a field, out in the open, doubtless believing themselves to be in no danger, three Stukas spotted them and went into screaming nosedives on their position. None of them rose to his feet again. Jeanne-Marie had kept his letters and a photograph of him in his gunner's uniform, in which he wears a somewhat embarrassed expression, as if to apologize in advance for his inglorious death and the promises of eternal love it had been so easy for him to keep. She had come to Paris in 1945 with her sister-in-law to meet up with one of her older brothers who had been taken prisoner in 1940, and was soon due to return to France with the flood of repatriated men. André Degorce had just come from Buchenwald. He was very weak, but the state of his health gave no great cause for concern and he was waiting at the Hôtel Lutetia reception centre to be reunited with his parents. Every day he consulted the listings. He tried to eat. He slept. He had no desire to live. One morning Jeanne-Marie Antonetti had appeared in the reception lobby at the Lutetia with her sister-in-law. She was seeking to be of use. Perhaps she also hoped that some miracle would restore her husband to her, ill but alive after all, and that all they would have to do would be to pick up the threads of their lost life together, just as easily as one wakes from a nightmare. She observed the concentration camp prisoners with a look of deep distress and when she caught André's eye she had burst into tears, saying over and over again: oh heavens, the poor little fellow. She went back to see him every day. She talked to him about her missing husband and her brothers, she was worried about the youngest of them, Marcel, mobilized in 1943, who must be somewhere in Germany, alive and well, she hoped, and she rejoiced to see how André was recovering his strength. Jean-Baptiste had finally turned up, in rude health. After a few months in a prison camp he had been lucky enough to be sent to a farm where he had lived off the fat of the land throughout the war. Jeanne-Marie had let him return to Corsica with his wife. She did not want to leave until André had found his parents and she stayed with him. On the night he undressed her she had drawn him to her, sighing, my little one, my child, and closed her eyes and let him have his way. Her skin was soft and cool and, if it no longer had the firmness of a girl's skin André would never know, for she was the first woman he had taken in his arms. A few months later they were married in Jeanne-Marie's village church. André's parents were not thrilled to see him marrying a woman much older than himself, but it seemed to him that what he had lived through authorized him to act without concerning himself over his parents' consent. All of Jeanne-Marie's family gazed with admiration at the uniform of the Saint-Cyr military academy in which he kneeled before the altar, his heart overflowing with gratitude to the Lord who delivers us from evil. After a year a daughter was born and when Marcel's wife died in childbirth somewhere on the banks of the river Niger, Jeanne-Marie had retrieved the little boy, so that he might receive the care her brother on his own could not give him and might not lack the feminine presence necessary for his later development. Marcel was due to take back his son, Jacques, later on, but he has not done so and never even mentions the possibility. Since his marriage Capitaine André Degorce seems to have spent much more of his time separated from his nearest and dearest than in their company. The children seem to him to have grown up in abrupt, erratic bursts. When he came home from Indochina after being imprisoned there, not weighing much more than when he was released from Buchenwald, he had difficulty in recognizing them and Jeanne-Marie wept to see him, as she had in the lobby of the Lutetia that spring morning in 1945. But he thought about them continually, and his conduct was always such that they need never blush at his name. He knows this is no longer the case today. He feels infinitely remote from them and yet is afraid lest in the end the dark stench of his sin might spread to them.

He observes firmly to the colonel, as the latter takes his leave, noisily ebullient with the success of his press conference, that he will not touch a hair of Tahar's head.

"No-one requires you to do so, Degorce," the colonel says drily.

"There would be no point, sir. There's no-one above him he could lead us to. It would really be quite pointless . . ."

"Very well. Do what you think best, Degorce. And keep me out of it. It's not my problem."

(*What a pathetic idiot. Pathetic, and a disgusting poseur.*)

Once the colonel has gone, he goes to see Tahar in his cell.

"I'm really sorry," Capitaine Degorce says. "It's too bad you had to go through all that. The press. The colonel."

Tahar starts to laugh.

"Yes," the capitaine says, laughing as well. "The colonel, especially, don't you think?"

He sits down facing Tahar.

"We won't touch you, you know."

"I ask no favours, capitaine. I'm ready to receive the same treatment as my comrades."

"It's not a favour. It's nothing to do with favours. It's a matter . . . a simple matter of logic, you see. You can't denounce yourself, can you?"

48

"I understand."

Capitaine Degorce remains silent for a long while. He feels curiously at peace and has no desire to leave.

"I have lived with you for long weeks, you know. I have your photograph in my office. I've been looking at you every day. It's strange to think it is all finished."

Tahar looks at the capitaine quizzically.

"But nothing is finished, capitaine. Nothing at all."

"How so? It's only a question of time now. You know that as well as I do."

"You're talking like your colonel," Tahar says softly. "The rebellion has been dealt a mortal blow, and all the rest of it. But that is not the truth."

"What is the truth?" the capitaine asks.

"The truth is simpler, capitaine," Tahar says, leaning towards him. "The truth is that I am finished, only me. And that is of no consequence. I count for nothing."

There is no element of drama in his voice, no inflexion hinting at any kind of vanity or the smallest craving for admiration. He has simply stated a fact and now he stretches out on the straw-filled mattress and closes his eyes with a sigh, as if preparing to sleep. The capitaine cannot help continuing to ponder on the mystery of his smile. He gets up.

"I'll come and see you tomorrow. If there's anything you need, don't hesitate to let me know."

"I need my freedom," Tahar says lightly.

"I meant anything that is within my power to give you."

49

"André, my child, my dear, we think about you such a lot. Our little Claudie never stops asking me if you could be with us for her birthday. Do you think you could? I know you'll do your best. It would make her so happy. And me, too. Write and tell me what I'm to say to her. It's a lovely day today and their uncle, Jean-Baptiste, has taken the children to the beach to eat sea urchins. So I've stayed at home with *Maman* and have found nothing to distract me from thinking about you, my dear. André, my child . . ."

Jeanne-Marie's words produce a totally disproportionate emotion in him, as if everybody he loves had died a thousand years ago and he had just discovered the last traces of their presence on earth. The future has been swept away and swallowed up, his wife is nothing but dust and from the depths of the grave she refers, with incredible cruelty, to the birthday of a little girl long since dead. Capitaine Degorce breaks off from reading. He glances distractedly through a letter from his parents, then another, from his brother-in-law Marcel, who, from his base on the banks of the hated river Niger, seems to have chosen him as the repository for his hypochondriac ravings, stubbornly deluging him with desperate missives, that seethe with abominable fauna, which he describes in disturbingly minute detail, parasites upon the eyes and liver, man-eating grubs, monsters lying in wait in the tropical humidity, Negroes possessed by spirits, and he unceasingly bewails his imminent death and the son he will never see. In each fresh letter Marcel explains how he has miraculously survived some disease, even though it was a killer, but the very same day has just identified the symptoms of yet another that really will carry him off, as a consequence of which, Capitaine Degorce has almost come to wish he would snuff it once and for all.

"André, my child, you cannot imagine how much I miss you. I often dream that this terrible business is over and done with and you're coming back home to us. I'm sure that day will come, soon perhaps. André, don't forget that your life is precious and . . ."

"Andreani's men are here, mon capitaine."

"I'll come at once. How many are they taking from us this evening?"

"Two, mon capitaine. The Kabylian and the Telemly girl."

Capitaine Degorce's prisoners are only transitory. After a few days or a few hours they make way for new ones coming in. They are taken away. They are removed to a transit camp. Or handed over to the public prosecutor. Or passed on to Lieutenant Andreani. Degorce does not know the rules that govern this selection. Perhaps there are no rules. There are so many prisoners it is impossible to deal with each one's case individually. It may be the work of a blind mechanism, as random and irremediable as fate. A canvas-topped lorry is parked in the empty street. It is very cold and the waning moon has a ring of mist around it. Andreani's men are chatting with Adjudant-chef Moreau. Capitaine Degorce recognizes the *harki* Belkacem and the little seminarist with a face like a weasel who acts as assistant to the lieutenant. They salute the capitaine, who responds with a vague nod of his head. They take Abdelkrim and the girl. Abdelkrim is shivering, with lowered eyes. The girl looks at the capitaine with an impenetrable expression. The lorry disappears into the darkness.

"That girl, mon capitaine," the adjudant-chef asks. "Do you think she's in for a good time over at Andreani's?"

"I've no idea, Moreau, and it's beside the point. What happens at Andreani's I can do nothing about."

*

"Don't forget, André, that your life is precious and we love you more than anything. Don't take pointless risks. Think of me. Think of us. And, please don't take this as any kind of reproach, but if you can find time to do so, please try to write us letters that are a bit longer and more detailed. Everything you do is of interest to us and the children especially would love . . ."

The capitaine can no longer concentrate on what he is reading. He is no longer upset. His mind finds it difficult to grasp the sense of the words and in the end he gives up. He puts the letter in a drawer with the one from his parents and tosses the one from Marcel into the waste paper basket. It seems to him that if he went to bed now he would be able to sleep, but he knows this is simply an illusion. He picks up a sheet of paper and begins to write. He tries to find words of tenderness but they elude him.

(There are no words left for God anymore. None for my loved ones.)

He opens the window and smokes a cigarette, gazing at the moon. He hopes Tahar is sleeping peacefully. And indeed does not doubt it for a second, thinking about his prisoner with vaguely envious resentment. He returns to his desk and, without even sitting down, he writes: "My darling, my adored children, I'm afraid it's inconceivable that I could get leave for Claudie's birthday. There's no special news here. Everything's going well. Fondest love." He scribbles Jeanne-Marie's address hastily on an envelope and throws it onto the pile of outgoing mail. In his bedroom he does not even take the trouble to kneel for his evening prayer. Sitting on the bed he opens his Bible. He reads: "What hast thou done? The voice of thy brother's blood crieth unto me from the ground." He leafs through it for a moment more and then closes it. He prepares to let himself drift between wakefulness and dreams he does not want.

How could I have forgotten you, mon capitaine, I who loved you so much, who loved you far more than I despise you today, even though I despise you to the extent of admitting unashamedly how much I loved you. Oh, I loved you like a brother, a dazzlingly youthful and heroic brother and I have a clear memory of your hand resting on my shoulder in May 1954 as we all marched together in a long, spectral troop beneath the eyes of our conquerors. It was the end of the world, we were no more than pitiful relics of a ruined empire, but your hand on my shoulder saved me from my despair at not having died in battle and I was happy, I clearly remember, happy to have remained alive and to be able to walk beside a man like you, who refused to lower your eyes, as all our comrades did, passing in front of the lens directed at us by Russian cameramen, so that the whole world might witness our humiliation and laugh at our former arrogance. For there was nothing left of our arrogance, mon capitaine, as we limped along, encrusted with mud and the camera's obscene eye made our wounds more painful and the bloody rags that had once been our battledress more repellent, there was nothing left of our courage, there was nothing left of us and, in truth, lowering our eyes was the only thing we could still do, but you, mon capitaine, as soon as we entered the camera's field of vision, you held your head high and stared at the lens and put your hand on my shoulder and said to me, Horace, hold your head high, and take a good look at these bastards, look them in the eye, you've nothing to be ashamed of, and I suddenly felt so proud, so proud to be at your side, that an unfathomable surge of joy almost took my breath away. I loved you, mon capitaine, and you seemed to me even more admirable then than I had ever dared to hope for, when listening to your brother-in-law, Jean-Baptiste Antonetti who, on the day before my parachute drop, was still talking about you in a particular bar in Hanoi that my Corsican compatriots used to frequent, to share their grudges and homesickness, the bar where I had spent such long weeks of waiting, drinking the vile spirit that marinated my dreams of battle and blood, my dreams of death, mon capitaine, while Jean-Baptiste talked of you, in between a couple of slurred allusions to the pitiless land of our childhood that we could not bring ourselves to loathe, and he talked about your strength and courage, and thanked heaven for allowing his sister to meet a man like you, as if his whole family had found itself abruptly ennobled by the mere fact of your presence, as if, through the mysterious blessing of being related to you, he himself had risen forever above his condition as a non-commissioned officer with an undistinguished career in the transport corps, and he said you would not die at Dien Bien Phu, for you were one of those people who survive the worst catastrophes, and doubtless, if he had had just one more drink, he would have ended up prophesying that you would live for ever. I spent so much time waiting to join you, mon capitaine, night after night in that bar in

Hanoi, as the pelting monsoon rains swept away all the dross of my bogus homesickness, I forgot my family, I shed everything that bound me to life, all that shackled me, I was making myself pure and available and I have never felt so wildly free as at that moment of climbing into the American troop transport that was at last going to carry me towards you. Your brother-in-law, Jean-Baptiste, clasped me to his heart, asking me to embrace you on his behalf and looked at me with the timid tenderness that is reserved for those who are already dead, but that did not disturb me and I settled down in the aircraft, strapped into my parachute harness, beside strangers as merry as if we had all been invited to a party. We no longer had faith in anything other than the pointless beauty of this sacrifice. The prospect of our impending deaths intoxicated us, and we were happy because we knew that this elation which made death desirable is the most blessed state men can aspire to. The first anti-aircraft salvoes shook the cabin, the door opened and we were flying so low that I smelt the sweet, humid smell of the massacre as I toppled into the liquid sky. I still recall my surprise and, I can tell you today, my disappointment, the first time I saw you, mon capitaine, I remember it clearly, Jean-Baptiste's tales had prepared me for an encounter with a kind of classical hero, with limbs of bronze, dipped in the dark waters of the Styx and not the youthful, melancholy lieutenant you were then, who seemed so frail, and I remember you gave a sad tilt of your head as you said, what the hell are you doing here? What's the point? It's all over, a ludicrous fuck-up, ludicrous and criminal, and I was hurt that you did not feel any gratitude towards those who had come to die with you, but then it is true that you have hurt me so many times, mon capitaine, without even being aware of it. I told you Jean-Baptiste embraced you. You replied that this message totally justified my presence and amid the hubbub and the stink you smiled at me. You called out to introduce me to the survivors in your section. This is sous-lieutenant Andreani, who's done us the honour of coming to share our fate. A caporal with a bandaged arm gave me a vague salute while continuing to fiddle with the radio. The others did not even glance at me. Our guns were firing shells at random through the mist into the side of an invisible mountain range, an implacably steady deluge of rain and steel streamed down on us and all around us the battlefield heaved like an appalling ocean of mud, with its eddies and the crests of its unmoving waves awash with a debris of flesh and metal. Very close to us a wounded man was groaning softly in a way that reminded me of the owl hooting in the August nights of my childhood. I heard yelling in every language under the sun. A dark hand groped upwards out of a mound of earth, as if reaching for something inconceivable. I tried to return your smile and I was still not afraid to die, but I did murmur, this is hell, I remember, this is hell, in a shaking voice, for which I have not forgiven myself and you said to me, no, this isn't hell, lieutenant, but it's the only hospitality on offer to you from Colonel de Castries' mistresses, Béatrice, Isabelle, Anne-Marie, Gabrielle, Claudine, Eliane, and all the other women who lingered in the memory of our commander to the extent that he had given their names to the positions upon which we were due to die, and what would they have thought, mon capitaine, all those women, whose faces we would never know, at the sight of their now aged lover taking his long aristocrat's nose and stooping figure for a walk along this maze of stinking trenches amid his army of living dead? How could they have recognized the man who used to meet them in secret in a light room with windows open onto the Parisian spring and crushed the scarlet waistcoat of his cavalry officer's uniform so boldly against their naked breasts. I thought about them so often during the incessant gunfire, I pictured their scented bodies reclining amid the warmth of their sheets, the caress of their hands and I felt as if the earth now swallowing us had retained something of them, as if the warm mud were like their arms, gently cradling the dying, before carrying them off into its voluptuous depths where nothing could reach them anymore, then it was so easy to fight, so tempting to die, and I do not understand how I can have forgotten which woman's name designated the position I fought to defend day and night at your side, was it Eliane, mon capitaine?, or was it Huguette? or Dominique? I no longer remember, I, who remember everything, have forgotten it, just as I have forgotten the name of the Algerian bride whose throat was cut years later, beside a long desert road between Béchar and Taghit, my memory refuses to retain women's names, that's how it is, mon capitaine, however much I think about them, their names fade away, and I no longer know if she was called Kahina, Latifa, or Wissam, but I know it was men who resembled your friend Tahar like brothers that killed her and scattered all the items from her wedding trousseau in the dust, frightful gilded high-heeled shoes, artificial silk underwear stitched with fake pearls, dresses embroidered in garish colours, all those pieces of excessively ornate silverware that were due to turn black at the bottom of a drawer in the married couple's home, but which the desert wind covered in sand. I read her name in the paper as I was drinking my whisky beneath the jasmine at the Hôtel Saint-George, just as I used to in the days of my merciless youth, and before summoning the taxi driver to take me to the childhood home I had invented for myself, I read her name, mon capitaine, swearing I would never forget it, but I can no longer remember it. She was not in her first youth, this I can remember clearly, she was a little over thirty and, as she sat there next to her husband in a brand new suit that was too tight for him, she was sweating beneath her make-up, while all the wedding guests clapped their hands and sang, I'd die for you, Sara, you are my life, Sara, she must have been blushing a little as she thought about her eagerness for her blood to flow at last, but not like that, not the way it did that night between Taghit and Béchar on that road we know so well. The world is old, mon capitaine, and we shall not escape from the stain of blood, we shall not be absolved of it, never, it is our curse and our greatness, it saddens me to have to say this to you again, for I probably first understood it on that crucial night at the age of sixteen, during the course of which what my life would be was revealed to me once and for all. It was late in the autumn of 1942, mon capitaine, I remember it clearly, and my cousin and I had found an Italian soldier wandering around the wretched patch in which my mother kept three puny chickens, he was scarcely older than us and he was shaking with fear, he was hungry, but we were so outraged that anyone should steal from us what little we had and so happy to find someone we could punish for our wretchedness, that we killed him unthinkingly with pickaxe blows, in a state of almost supernatural elation. We dragged his body as far from our house as possible, outside the village. He had on him a photograph of a girl with an unattractive face and a couple of letters which we tore up without reading them. We took his gun, his wallet, his identity disc and his hand grenades and we ran to join the *maquis* at Alta Rocca, we ran until we were breathless and my cousin began wailing, what have we done, Horace? What will become of us? but I did not answer him because it was of no interest to me. My hands were marked with blood and the life I had known was over. I felt neither joy nor regret. I was content to keep running and I knew I should follow this road to the end, suppressing the murmurings of my heart, and I followed it, mon capitaine, I followed it up to September 1943 on the ridge at Bacinu, where the machine guns of the S.S. Reichsführer Division mowed my cousin down, there close beside me, only allowing him to pass on to me, by way of farewell, a little of his blood on my cheek, I followed it to the pocket of resistance at Colmar in January 1945, and all the way to Germany, and across the seas, beneath the monsoon, I followed it all the way to you, mon capitaine, you whom I loved so well. I looked at you and I thought it would be enough for me to die here for my life to be perfect. Oh, you were admirable, mon capitaine, it is hard for me to admit it today but it is the truth, you were haloed by an aura of grace, the purest grace, in every one of your actions. The Vietnamese sappers dug circular tunnels around our positions to isolate and destroy them, one after the other, Anne-Marie, Marcelle, Eliane, and every day voices came over the radio from unknown comrades saying, it's finished, goodbye boys, goodbye, voices filled with sadness and fury, to which we used to answer, chin up, good-bye, goodbye, as we awaited our turn, and when our turn came you simply asked, why make their task easy for them? and we crawled towards the wet sound of spades digging rhythmically into the earth gorged with water, we hurled our grenades before slithering after you into the tunnel and fought hand to hand, with our fists, with knives, with our teeth, borne along by a marvellous euphoria that I would never forget. As we caught our breath we were able to see that the ones we had just killed were no more than fifteen or sixteen years old. They lay there in the mud, thin and frail, and death made them look like little children, each face twisted in a wilful pout. We blew up the props, the clay engulfed the bodies and we withdrew. Every day we began again and each time I had the feeling that, with a pounding heart, I, too, was about to encounter an adored mistress who would soon yield. When General Giap's headquarters granted us a respite by selecting another target, you shook our hands, again murmuring, that's right, why make their task easy? and you went and sat down a little apart from us, with your eyes closed. No, it was not hell, and I was filled with a great love for every one of the weary men falling asleep around me in filthy, sodden blankets, and above all for you, my brother, for it was from you they derived their strength and their strange beauty, and I knew that, without you, they would fade away, like stars that have lost their heat. Do not be offended, please, I have the right to call you my brother, mon capitaine, we were sired together by the same battle under the monsoon rains, the same ghosts of loving women hovered over us, and that is how I still want to address you. Some things cannot be undone, even by contempt. I loved your solitariness and silence, my brother, I loved your gaiety, I even came to love your piety, I who knew that the vast heavens above the monsoon clouds were empty and the universe blind, yet I went to Mass with you and we listened in the rain to the crazed chaplain's sermon, as he raised his chalice aloft behind an altar made of planks and rusty trestles, indifferent to the screaming of the 105 mm shells, and I watched the pallid backs of the officers' necks as they all bowed forward together, as if the weight of an invisible caress were gently pressing them down towards the earth. I tried to guess what you might be praying for. What could still be granted to us? We were a stricken beast, vast and vulnerable, all of whose flesh had been torn away, piece by piece, but stubbornly they continued to parachute useless reinforcements in to us from Hanoi that descended from the heavens along with myriad medals and mentions in despatches, love letters written by unknown women, notices of promotion, bottles of champagne, the glittering star thanking Colonel de Castries for allowing his name and those of the women he had loved to remain forever associated with this slaughter, the stripes they awarded you and the second gilded medal bar by which I was granted the privilege of dying in the skin of a regular army lieutenant, and all the other trivia that lit up our death agony like fireworks. The day the order to cease fire reached us, silence fell upon us all at once in the afternoon, I clearly remember. I was not dead and had forgotten what silence was. My life suddenly lost its justification. We had destroyed our weapons and tied up a few effects in pieces of parachute fabric. The Viet Minh emerged from the mist. They assembled us on what had been the airfield, amid craters filled with dark water, and divided us up by rank. The Russians set up their cameras. A little further on Général de Castries was getting into a lorry with a group of senior officers. For weeks we marched through the jungle beneath a vault of immense trees whose crowns had been tied together with ropes, we crossed rivers, walked through villages where spittle rained down on us, passing, without stopping, wounded men seated beside the road, who looked at us with eyes already empty and cold as mirrors, and you understood well before I did, mon capitaine, that they had been abandoned there by our own comrades, you understood this at once and I saw the anguish settling into your face as you kept saying to me, take care, Horace, now more than ever, you don't know what you're going to have to contend with, and we went on marching all the way to the re-education camp, faster and faster, leaving our own men to die on the way. There were no barbed wire fences, only the darkness of the jungle. Little mounds of earth could be seen more or less everywhere. Skeletal French soldiers, survivors of the Route Coloniale 4 battalion, could be seen lying on a soaking tarpaulin. We formed a group of some forty junior officers and it was the end of the world. Nothing bound us to one another anymore. I could not bear it. The possibility of survival had replaced the certainty of death and it was mutating into a greedy, imperious longing, an abject longing that swept away everything, courage, the dignity of hope, a shared past, and from the first day I had to listen to Capitaine Lestrade, who shaved himself carefully every morning with a fragment of a blade to preserve his honour as a French officer, advising us to agree to the proposal made by the Viet Minh that the weight of the allocations of rice should be calculated according to rank. You simply announced, almost in a murmur, that you had never had much of an appetite and that whatever decision were taken you would be satisfied with an ordinary private's ration. I said it would be the same for me. A sous-lieutenant whose gleaming new insignia proclaimed that he had just been promoted, said, me too, a private's ration, and, from his accent I immediately identified him as a fellow Corsican. After a moment other voices spoke up, but I knew they would have remained comfortably silent if you had not spoken, and Capitaine Lestrade quietly lowered his eyes. I went over to see the sous-lieutenant and asked him where he came from. He was called Paul Mattei, you must remember, mon capitaine, and as you shook his hand I could see Capitaine Lestrade giving you a look filled with shame and resentment. Did he have time to think about the baseness, the futility of all that, Capitaine Lestrade, did he have time to reflect that a few extra grains of rice would have made no difference to him, did he have time, mon capitaine? before we dug his grave less than three weeks later, in driving rain, our muscles frozen from having had to use spades so often, to dig so many graves, that of Lieutenant Thomas, that of Lieutenant Maury de la Ribière, those of all the men who hoped to live, but who had allowed themselves to be so trapped by the mirages of thirst that they lapped up dirty water like dogs, which forced them to drag themselves to the latrines twenty times a day until they no longer had the strength to do it and died one after another in putrid puddles of blood and mucus, still dreaming in their fever of the day of our liberation, and as we thrust them into the ditch, one after another, you would repeat to me, mon capitaine, that such was man, stripped naked, and that his weakness was such that he did not deserve our hatred, and I admired your unfailing benevolence even if I could neither share nor understand it, for truly it was more than I could bear and without you, I should not have survived, I am not sure if I should thank you for it, but I know I should not have survived, the rage that constantly made me choke would have killed me in the end, I felt its heat overcoming me at the sight of the corpses we buried in the rain, its crimson mists obscured my vision at each of the re-education sessions, during which we had to submit to the implacable speeches of the political commissar about the meaning of history and the coming of the new man, as if the new man were not already there, in front of him, at this very moment, thin and stinking, his loose teeth awash in the sewer of his gums, as he had always been since the beginning of the world and as he will be for ever, you know as well as I do, mon capitaine, but the political commissar went on uttering the same idiocies and I was literally shaking with rage at his Jesuitical grimaces, his understanding, ruthless smile, his schoolmasterly manner, he revolted me so much I could not hold back from telling him that what the communists had instituted was no more than an international of filth, I could not hold back, and it gave me untold relief to say it to him, hoping, perhaps, that he would have me shot and that the whole intolerable charade would come to an end, but he merely looked at me with a sorrowful expression, which increased my fury, and that evening when the soldier who distributed the food got to me he threw my rice down into the mud soiled with bloody diarrhoea. You offered me half your ration, how could I forget it, mon capitaine? and I said to you, no, André, don't do that, think of yourself, but you gave me a wink and declaimed, man does not live by bread alone, and burst out laughing, I clearly remember, I was not afraid of fasting, I dreamed of getting rid of all my organs, of hurling my intestines twisted by cramps far away from me, my heart and my liver, I dreamed of drying up the source of the fluids I persisted in secreting in spite of myself, so as to become clean and dry like dead wood, but you gave me a wink and I burst out laughing. Paul Mattei sat down beside us and all three of us shared our food while the others were sucking their balls of rice and looking the other way as they slowly rolled them around in their mouths until they dissolved. Oh, I loved you so much, mon capitaine, and if I had not been so totally blinded by love I should have died there, I should have thrown your rice back in your face and I should not have allowed myself to be persuaded to complete my self-criticism and publicly express my gratitude to Ho Chi Minh, so that the political commissar condescended to give the order for me to be fed once more, because all that I loved in you was simply the mask for inordinate pride, mon capitaine, you were not an idiot like Lestrade, you knew that your honour did not depend on shaving every day, but the lofty idea you had of yourself demanded that you should constantly act out the masquerade of fraternity and self-denial, which you had no difficulty in doing for, the truth is that you were as if on your home ground in that camp, you acted out the role you were born to play there and at which you excelled, it must be admitted, because you had been preparing for it all your life, and if you could hold forth on the subject of man stripped naked over the bodies of Lestrade, Maury de la Ribière and Thomas, who had been finished off by the repellent spectacle of their own nakedness more surely than by dysentery, it was because you yourself felt secure within the comforting armour plating of your pride. I do not doubt for a second that you would have died rather than stoop to the most insignificant pettiness, and God knows I loved you for that, mon capitaine, although in the end it is so easy to die, it is a task everyone invariably achieves, which should cause no great wonder, everyone knows how to die, torturers and martyrs, heroes and cowards, naive young brides and little nine-year-old bridesmaids, oh, no, I don't doubt that you would have known how to die with panache and dignity, but nothing disgusts me more than men self-obsessed to the point of worrying about how to die with dignity, men like you, mon capitaine, who devote all their efforts to the staging of their own lives right up to the final apotheosis, I imagine the bride from Taghit must have wept and lamented in vain in the desert, my little seminarist may have called out for his mother and begged the God he no longer believed in to come to his aid, your friend Tahar himself would certainly have disappointed you if you could have been present at his end, they all died horribly, as men die, and this is totally unimportant, we have never needed men who know how to die, we need men who know how to conquer, men capable of unhesitatingly sacrificing all that is most precious to them, their own hearts, their souls, to victory, mon capitaine, yet while you have never feared death, the prospect of victory has filled you with indescribable terror and finally stripped you naked, in your turn, for the first time in your life, in those dank cellars in Algeria where the trembling nakedness of your prisoners reflected your own image back at you, without your being able to shield yourself from it. You are wrong, mon capitaine, I know this now, weakness well deserves our hatred, above all when it must be paid for at the exorbitant price of a further defeat and I cannot forgive you, not even in the name of the love I bore you, which blinded me for so long it is impossible for me to forget it, for I so loved you that I was happy at first, when they started giving me my rice again, that you no longer had to deprive yourself of food on my account. In the end the Viet Minh added scraps of meat and pieces of fruit to our rations, which we ate with relish, without even trying to understand what had earned us this privilege. Paul Mattei said, they're going to release us, they're trying to plump us up a bit, they're going to release us. I realized that for a long time I had no longer been thinking about release. I had gradually settled down into a world whose limits did not extend beyond those of the present moment. I sat close to you on the floor of the lorry that was taking us back towards our people, towards a world so vast that it had totally forgotten us. In the villages no-one spat at us anymore. Before handing us over to the French soldiers, the political commissar came and shook us by the hand and none of us refused. Military doctors took charge of us and it was only when I saw their looks that I grasped the extent of my physical deterioration. From our group there were twenty-seven survivors. We shared out between us the task of writing to the families of the dead and it fell to me to bear witness to the death of Capitaine Lestrade and those of Lieutenants Thomas and Maury de la Ribière. You asked me, I clearly recall, Horace, do you feel yourself capable of writing these letters as they should be written? I replied that I would do it and I did it, remember, I always knew there was something in loyalty that was infinitely superior to truth. We found your brother-in-law Jean-Baptiste again, in the bar in Hanoi he never seemed to have stirred from as he waited to greet you, and we drank without raising our glasses to anything, the spirit burned me, I allowed myself to succumb to hopeless drunkenness, like the end of the world, and whores vibrant with patriotism wound their incredibly fleshy arms about our necks, Paul Mattei buried his face in the breasts of a laughing girl and I could hear your voice saying timidly, forgive me, don't be offended, while Jean-Baptiste was assuring you that he would not breathe a word to his sister and you kept saying, no, that's not the point, and I stopped thinking about you, mon capitaine, I hugged the girl to me and asked her her name which she murmured as she slid the tip of her tongue from my ear to the corner of my mouth, but I did not want to kiss her, the continuous bleeding of my gums left a taste of metal in my mouth that I was ashamed of, I touched her buttocks through her dress and inhaled her perfume, in the depths of which the sugary scent of corpses still lingered, and then she took me into a room where I had to learn the taste of living flesh again. For a long time I rested my head against her belly which was as pliant as mud, lost amid the mists of the alcohol, I managed to catch hold of her ankle, and when my fingers brushed against her foot I heard her suppressing a little amused laugh. I asked her her name again and she repeated it in loud, clear tones which echoed in the darkness, she repeated it, but, you see, mon capitaine, I cannot recall it.

28 MARCH, 1957: SECOND DAY
Matthew xxv, 41-43

Every morning the shame of being oneself must be discovered anew. But, before this, the grace of a secret respite is granted. The night's dream disintegrates, leaving nothing more in Capitaine André Degorce's heart than a vague premonition of grief to come. He has no past, no family, no name. He simply lies there on his bed, his eyes open upon the light of a dawn he does not recognize. As yet nothing exists in this world apart from the incredibly calming image of Tahar, seated on his straw mattress, his feet and hands shackled, smiling at something invisible. Capitaine Degorce would like to go on enjoying this sweet obliviousness, but he cannot stop himself wondering who this man is and then he remembers brutally. The recollection is pitiless.

(*I am a jailer, his jailer.*)

Seated on the edge of his bed, he surveys his bare legs with disgust, goose pimples everywhere, the hairs standing up on the livid skin of his thighs. He dresses with the feeling of hiding a loathsome secret from view and gulps down a large cup of tepid coffee which makes him feel nauseous. He smokes several cigarettes at the open window, sucking in the damp, cold air. A yellow glow lights up the horizon and the call to dawn prayers arises from the Casbah. When the muezzin has fallen silent the sun appears above the city's apartment buildings. Capitaine Degorce paces along empty corridors. He hears murmuring and moans from behind the doors of the cells. Two *harkis* are energetically cleaning the floor in one of the interrogation rooms. Adjudant-chef Moreau sits on the corner of a table, and seems absorbed in the glum contemplation of the ceramic friezes at the corner of the ceiling – sinuous stylized flower patterns, yellow, green and blue, which look strangely dull under the harsh brilliance of the electric light bulb. One of the *harkis* lets his mop fall in order to stand to attention, the other steadies it to his side, doing what he can to adopt a more or less regulation position. Degorce signals to them to carry on and goes to shake the hand of Moreau who has stood up to salute him.

"How's things, mon capitaine? Would you like some coffee? We have some freshly made."

The capitaine consents as he watches the foaming of the grey water across the tiles.

"Thank you, Moreau. What I've just been drinking was really vile."

He follows the adjudant-chef into a little room arranged as a makeshift kitchen. They drink their coffee in silence. Capitaine Degorce pulls a face as he sets his cup down.

"This is vile, too. But, at least it's hot."

Moreau smiles faintly.

"May I have your permission to speak about something, mon capitaine?"

"That's the stupidest question I've ever heard, Moreau," Capitaine Degorce remarks good-humouredly. "How do you expect me to tell if I can give you permission if I don't know what it's about?

Speak anyway. I'll soon tell you if you'd have done better to keep your mouth shut."

Moreau extracts a crumpled packet of Gitanes from his pocket. He takes out two cigarettes and smoothes them for a long time before offering one to the capitaine. He explores his pockets again in search of a box of matches.

"Spit it out, man!" says the capitaine impatiently, offering his lighter.

Moreau still takes the time to inhale deeply.

"It's about Febvay."

"Febvay?"

"Sergent Febvay, mon capitaine."

"Well? Do you mean you still haven't banished him to Tamanrasset for me?" Capitaine Degorce asks, hating the falsely assumed casual tone he can hear in his own voice.

Moreau pointedly refrains from smiling and stares attentively at him, drawing on his cigarette.

(*I'm no longer good for anything. Nothing at all.*)

"The thing is, mon capitaine, I'd like you to reconsider your decision. I don't think it's fair. Febvay is a good fellow."

"A good fellow," Capitaine Degorce repeats. "A good fellow."

He forces himself to recall the revolver thrust into the girl's vagina, the sergent's laughing face and repeats again, almost in a murmur: "A good fellow . . ." hoping that anger would come to his aid and let him get carried away, but nothing happens. He does not even manage to feel concerned.

(*I simply ought to be somewhere else, somewhere else.*)

He closes his eyes for a moment and the words come.

"I don't propose to discuss your quite fascinating conception of what constitutes a good fellow, Moreau, because it doesn't interest me and because it's beside the point, do you see, it's totally beside the point. Let me brief you on what's at stake here and when you've understood this clearly yourself perhaps you'll be able to back me up effectively by making sure the men never forget it, instead of trying my patience with reports on your early morning cogitations. *What's at stake*, Moreau, is the sense of our mission. *What's at stake* is what justifies it and it's very simple, really very simple. What we do here only makes sense because it's effective. It's only acceptable from a moral point of view because it's effective. It enables us to save lives . . . innocent lives. Effectiveness is our only goal and that's what sets our . . . limits. If we lose sight of effectiveness . . ."

"But, mon capitaine, we don't . . ."

"Be quiet when I'm speaking, adjudant-chef, be quiet!" says Capitaine Degorce crisply, fully aware that he has found his authority again. "Confine yourself to paying attention and keeping quiet until I tell you to speak. So, if we lose sight of effectiveness, if we allow people like Febvay to run amok and take perverse pleasure, lubricious pleasure, in the . . . in the operations of . . . the process, we are no longer soldiers fulfilling their mission, we're . . . I don't know what we are. I don't even want to think about it. Do you understand?"

"Yes, mon capitaine. I understand. What Febvay did was out of order. Totally out of order. And I was totally out of order in letting him do it."

"I'm not obliging you to say this, Moreau. And don't make too much of that aspect of the problem."

Capitaine Degorce pours himself another cup of coffee without taking his eyes off Moreau. He has just found honourable and rational motivation for behaviour which, the previous day, at the moment when he totally lost control of himself, was motivated by nothing more than frayed nerves caught on the raw.

But the most troubling thing is that the line of argument that absolved and justified him, was not even something he had to fashion for himself, it was already there, immediately to hand, he has heard it a hundred times in the mouths of his superiors and all he had to do was to take it up for his own use with equal fluency and conviction, reproducing it even down to the calculated hesitations, circumlocutions and euphemisms, and for these, since he did not invent them, all he had to do was to let the powerful tide flow through him, like foul water along a sewer, a tide of words whose impeccably logical sequence required neither his input nor his assent. Yet every time he has himself heard this line of reasoning being advanced, notably in the robust version of it favoured by the colonel, he has experienced an extraordinary revulsion, shuddering with disgust at every word uttered, not so much because there was a brazen lie within it, but because at the very heart of this brazen lie, expression was being given to the purest, the most undeniable truth, a truth over which he had no control and which held them all, Moreau, Febvay, the colonel and himself in its icy grip.

"It was out of order, I know, mon capitaine," Moreau repeats. "But we all screw up at times. We're all human."

Capitaine Degorce makes no reply.

(*We're all human. But that's the fault, not the excuse. The fault.*)

"It's not easy here," pleads Moreau again. "It's the arsehole of the world here."

"To the best of my knowledge," says Capitaine Degorce, "and to take up your elegant metaphor, the world has a number of arseholes."

Moreau smiles weakly.

"So what about it, mon capitaine?" he asks. "He's already felt the weight of your fist in his face. Couldn't that be enough? Please."

Capitaine Degorce knows he risks nothing now by appearing magnanimous. He couldn't give a damn about Febvay. If he gets rid of him they'll give him another Febvay. Men have lost all that used to make them unique, for good or ill. They are all alike.

"Very well, Moreau. Tell Febvay the incident is closed. And tell him to keep out of my way in the corridor over the next few days. To give me time to calm down completely."

Adjudant-chef Moreau lays a grateful hand on his arm.

"Thank you, mon capitaine, thank you."

For a moment Capitaine Degorce wonders why Moreau is so keen to keep Febvay at his side, for the sake of what shared past, what blind affection, what fatherly protective impulse. He could try to find out, he could have a heart to heart talk with Moreau, break out of the glutinous straitjacket that restricts him, speak words that are really his own, but once again he feels overcome by a longing to be somewhere else, somewhere, he now realizes, where he should have been since he woke up.

"Let's just say that I'm doing this for you, Moreau."

"Thank you, mon capitaine."

Capitaine Degorce leaves the room, saying, "I'm going to look in on Hadj Nacer." He takes a few steps, and turns back towards the adjudant-chef.

"Do you need me this morning?"

"I've got some leads to follow up, mon capitaine. An individual to bring in. But I can look after all that on my own."

*

He squats unmoving on his mattress, as in Degorce's dream, but he is so tranquil one could believe him to be seated in the cool shade of a palm grove at Timimoun or Taghit, watching the undulation of the dunes caressed by a warm wind, beyond the filthy wall, absorbed in the contemplation of sweet and mysterious things that belong to him alone.

"Good morning," says Capitaine Degorce, stopping himself at the last minute from saying, "Did you sleep well?"

Tahar greets him with a tilt of his head.

"I have no news concerning you. I shall certainly have some during the course of the morning."

"It's not important," Tahar says.

The capitaine remains standing for a moment before sitting down facing his prisoner. He feels obliged to explain his presence, he searches for some kind of pretext, but can find nothing to say apart from the truth and the simplicity of this truth gives him an immense feeling of well being.

"If you are willing to do so . . . I wanted to have a conversation with you. If you are willing. I don't want to intrude on you."

"We can talk, capitaine," says Tahar. "We can talk."

Capitaine Degorce relaxes and leans back against the damp wall, with half-closed eyes. "I'm not at peace with myself," he says softly and adds in even quieter tones, as if to himself, "Not at peace at all . . ." A painful emotion weighs upon his chest. He could have said these words to Jeanne-Marie, instead of persisting in writing to her in the same set phrases, the only ones his mind is apparently capable of producing now and at the cost of such a painful effort whenever he tries to address his wife and children, and of course Jeanne-Marie would not have judged him, on the contrary, she would have preferred a thousand times to be sharing his torments and doubts, instead of wearing out the patience of her love against the ramparts he has erected around his heart, day after day, a heart filled with silence, or he could have sought an interview with the colonel and spoken these same words to him, without beating about the bush, as befits a free man on whom his actions confer the inalienable right to express himself as he likes, and what would it matter to him if that idiot did not understand him or bawled him out or threatened to place him under arrest? He had no need of the colonel's respect, but above all, he should first have spoken those words to himself, confronted them on his own, and gauged the fearful weight of them, he should have taken thought before incurring the guilt of such a terrible transgression by uttering them here, face to face with a man in chains whom he has spent weeks hunting down and who remains his enemy, a man who has ordered the deaths of innocent civilians, and armed those who killed them, on a number of occasions, who has sown death and terror and who seems as serene and easy as if all this spilled blood were no more important than a rainstorm blown away by the wind. And it is for this reason, Degorce knows it well, that these words can only be spoken to him.

"I understand," murmurs Tahar.

The softness of his voice suddenly makes Capitaine Degorce horribly ill at ease.

"No," he says in firm tones. "I'm not at peace. And so, you see, when I told you yesterday that it's all finished, I was not seeking to impress you or anything, I was not being triumphalist, not at all. I said it because it's true, it's finished. It's only a matter of time. If you come into my office you'll see it for yourself at once. You'll see the organization chart, your organization has been almost entirely dismantled, its total dismantling is inevitable, truly, and so, it's finished. But this victory, this victory . . ." The capitaine shrugs. ". . . I suppose there must be some less painful victories, victories one can be proud of. Well, let's say this is not one of them and I should personally have preferred to have had no part in it."

He lights two cigarettes and offers one to Tahar.

"Why?" Tahar asks with genuine interest. "I don't believe in your victory at all. But if you are sure of it, why?"

"You know why," says Capitaine Degorce.

"No, I don't know," insists Tahar. "Tell me."

Capitaine Degorce waves the smoke away with an open hand and takes refuge in silence for a moment.

"You know," he finally says, "I was in the Resistance –" and holds back from adding, stupidly, "As well." "And I was arrested. In 1944. Arrested and interrogated."

He has confessed this dozens of times, in confident tones, to Algerian prisoners, as he did only the previous day to Abdelkrim, seeking out weak spots, each time seizing the right moment to establish an apparent human contact with the man being spoken to, either so as to lead him to think that what he has just suffered was commonplace and trivial, or on the other hand to let him glimpse a feigned weakness which might encourage fresh trust, without his realizing that such trust would be his undoing. Capitaine Degorce has learned to modulate his declaration, adopting the tone most appropriate to his chosen goal, donning a mask now of compassion, now of spinelessness, now of arrogant disdain, and on each occasion he has concentrated on this goal to the extent of forgetting that he was talking about events that had actually taken place. But today there is not this goal and for the first time the words send him back to the Gestapo command post in Besançon, where two men, whose faces he has forgotten, but not the smell of their tobacco and eau de cologne, stroll slowly round him, rolling up their sleeves with fastidious care in the June heat. He understands the intent of their theatrical display and tries to breathe steadily without following them with his eyes, but he cannot control the thumping of his heart. A few weeks before, when Charles Lézieux, his mathematics teacher in the senior preparatory class, agreed to entrust him with his first mission of clandestine billposting, a pathetic mission, he said to him: "If you have the misfortune to be caught, André, don't seek to play the hero. Try to say nothing for twenty-four hours. Twenty-four hours. That will be enough." Tied to a chair, as the two men prowl round him with the calm assurance of predators, André Degorce only asks himself one thing: will he be able to hold out for twenty-four hours? This question totally absorbs him, prevents him thinking about his parents' loving care, his dreams of winning a place at the Ecole Normale Supérieure, his long walks after school on spring evenings beside the river Doubs in the company of Lézieux, the laughing eyes of an unknown schoolgirl whom he will never meet again, the gentle warmth of the midnight Masses of his childhood, all the things whose memory is waiting to slip into his soul and move him and bend it until it breaks under the weight of sadness and when one of the men finally strikes him with his hand and the signet ring he wears bursts open his lip, he is almost relieved because he knows the answer will come soon. Yes, it is a real relief, he remembers it clearly, because hope and fear have been brutally driven out by the supreme intervention of physical pain which also dislocates memory, thought and time, but the answer will not come, it has never come, each moment has been curiously nullified or extended, one second following another second, they are absorbed into nothingness, where they congeal to form eternity and twenty-four hours is now utterly meaningless. Capitaine André Degorce again sees him-self naked, lying on the ground, his knees pressed back into his chest, no longer knowing what part of his body to protect, there is an uncanny slowness about the way the two men lean over him, he can smell them, feel the heat of their breath, there is an electric light bulb, a bare wire, the grey china of a bath, a sky overhead of soapy water that tastes of blood and suddenly he is alone, breathing greedily, a hand is pulling at his hair, he has emptied his bowels beneath him, he hears an unhappy voice saying disapprovingly, you're really a swine, young man, a filthy swine, where were you brought up? His broken ribs are making him wail like a newborn baby, but he can no longer feel any pain, pain has become the intimate stuff of his being and he is delaying the confessional moment from second to second, the delicious moment when he will be able to say the name of his mathematics teacher, the only name he knows, he delays it until, without his having said anything, they lock him up in a cell, from which he only emerged to be sent to Buchenwald. At the transit camp, he finally learned that ten days had elapsed since his arrest, but he has never known how much time the interrogation lasted. On the station platform the scents of summer and the vastness of the sky make him giddy and when the van doors close on him all the memories of his youth, which the dominance of the pain had so far kept at arm's length, come flooding in all together, they melt into one another and become concentrated into a single feeling, one of absolute simplicity, the poignant feeling of life's sweetness, he is nineteen, sobs choke in his throat and if at that moment someone had promised him he could return home and see his mother again, he would have told them all they wanted to know. His Gestapo torturers ought to have known that, they should have granted him the respite that would have opened his soul to them, but they could not care less about what he did or did not confess, they only wanted to test and punish him. They had no need of intelligence because Charles Lézieux had been arrested an hour before him, just as he was getting ready to meet André, and there had never been any secret to protect.

During all these years he has never really thought about any of that again; the wars he has fought in did not leave him time to do so and the ten months spent in Buchenwald extend behind him like a vast grey steppe that cuts his life in two and separates it for ever from the lost continent of his youth, but he has not forgotten it. June 1944 silently left its mark in his flesh, inscribing there the imprint of an unforgettable lesson, one that has enabled him to explain to his N.C.O.s: "Remember this, gentlemen, pain and fear are not the only keys for opening the human soul. They are sometimes ineffective. Don't forget that there are others. Homesickness. Pride. Sadness. Shame. Love. Take note of the person in front of you. Don't be pointlessly stubborn. Find the key. There's always a key –" and he has now arrived at the absurd and intolerable conviction that he was only arrested at the age of nineteen so as to learn how to fulfil a mission that would be entrusted to him in Algeria thirteen years later. But this he cannot say to Tahar.

"You were interrogated yourself in 1944," Tahar repeats. "Yes, now I understand."

His attentive and sincerely distressed face exasperates Capitaine Degorce. "It's your methods!" he says drily. "It's your methods that force us to . . ." He stubs out his cigarette on the ground and tosses the end into a corner of the cell. "You leave us no choice!" he says and once more restrains himself from adding at the last moment, "What do you expect us to do?"

"That's strange," Tahar murmurs meditatively.

"What's strange?"

"Yes, it's strange," Tahar continues. "You see, I was sure it was we who had no choice about our methods."

Capitaine Degorce looks at him for a long time.

(*Logic can be turned inside out, like a glove. Lies. Truth.*)

He has regained his composure. He no longer wants to talk about the war. They have taken Tahar's shoes away and he is wearing darned socks. Capitaine Degorce is bizarrely troubled by this.

"I haven't asked you: would you like tea or coffee? Would you like a wash? I must warn you, the coffee's foul ..."

A soldier comes into the cell: "You must come, mon capitaine, it's the colonel on the phone." Degorce stands up.

"I'll come back," he says to Tahar.

He turns to the soldier: "You will remain with ..." He does not know how to refer to Tahar. He does not want to say "the prisoner", nor to use his *nom de guerre* or refer to him as "*Monsieur*". "What is your rank in the A.L.N.?" he asks Tahar.

"I'm a colonel in the A.L.N."

"You will remain with Colonel Hadj Nacer," he resumes. "Make sure he has everything he needs. And give him back his shoes, if he wishes."

*

"You've landed us in deep shit, Degorce, do you know that? Are you aware of that? I hope you had a vile night, a really vile night, like me. What the hell are we going to do with your Hadj Nacer? I swear I'd have liked it better if he'd put up a bit of a fight when he was arrested, the bloody bastard, that would have suited us very well, I'm telling you ..."

"I don't understand, sir. Yesterday you were very pleased."

"Well, there you are, that's life, my friend. First people are pleased and then they're not ... That's the way it is ... You put on your thinking cap ... you see things in a different light ... Aspects you hadn't considered ... complications ... Good God, man, it's not hard to understand! Do you never think things over yourself?"

(*The cretin has had a bollocking.*)

"On occasion, sir."

"How is he, Hadj Nacer? Depressed?"

"You saw him yesterday, sir. No, he's not depressed. Certainly not."

"And what about security? There's no risk of him escaping? Or trying?"

"No, sir."

"Are you sure? Absolutely sure?"

"Yes, sir. Absolutely."

"Good ... Good ... Very good ..."

"When do you want me to hand him over for trial, sir? Once that's done, it's no longer our problem."

"I don't need your opinion, Degorce. I'll ring you later today to give you your instructions."

*

87

The morning post. Jeanne-Marie. His parents. Marcel. Capitaine Degorce fingers the envelopes and again that vision of Claudie appears, so clear this time: she lies there on a bed with heavy white sheets, her nostrils pinched in her pallid little face, her eyes ringed with blue shadows and a rosary wrapped round her stiff fingers. All about her are her grandparents, her uncles and aunts, her mother, holding Jacques by the hand, and even Marcel, who has somehow or other escaped from his African hell and is in rude health: the only one missing is himself and his absence is so natural that nobody notices it. Perhaps he is still in Algeria, perhaps in a room next door, detained there in perpetuity by his guilt. His morbid fantasies have become a matter of habit, they no longer genuinely distress him, even though he cannot help indulging in them.

(*My God, my God, what a tragedy* . . .)

He opens the letters and glances through them one after the other.

"André, my child, my dearest, Claudie and Jacques have been particularly tiresome today, they really need . . ."

"My dear son, your father's health, which until now . . ."

". . . and this time I'm having these frightful attacks of diarrhoea that give me no respite and exhaust me terribly . . ."

What is the point of all this news? In what way does it still concern him? What can he do about it? He would prefer to receive no more letters. Nor to write any more. He would like to be taken back to the spring of 1955 at the hotel in Piana. His clothes still hung loosely about him, his stomach gave him pain every time he ate food that was a little too rich, but the sky was so bright. Claudie had twisted her ankle running on the beach and he had gently massaged her foot as she watched him, making little grimaces of pain from time to time to which he responded with self-pitying exclamations that made her burst out laughing.

"... and we send you all our love ..."

"... André, you are so dear to us ..."

At Piana his heart was not empty. He was not ashamed of himself.

"... and maggots in my eyes, live maggots, flowing like tears."

*

A little Arab boy of about ten is sitting on a bench in the corridor. A soldier squatting in front of him is doing conjuring tricks for him. A five-franc piece disappears from his hand, to reappear in his mouth or behind the ear of the child, whose eyes open wide.

"Who is this lad?" Capitaine Degorce asks.

"He's the son of a suspect, mon capitaine."

Moreau emerges from the interrogation room and takes the capitaine aside a little.

"The one I picked up this morning, mon capitaine, he talked. Solid stuff, I think."

"He's talked? Already?"

"Yes, mon capitaine, but it wasn't all that difficult, you know. He's a hefty fellow, very moody. So I got them to bring out the generator, the electrodes, the whole kit, under his nose. I asked one of the lads to connect up to see if it was all working. They brought a bucket of water and sponges and I explained to the fellow that in my opinion, tough guy as he was, there would be no point in our getting rough with him. I said I was sure he was brave and wouldn't talk, well, you get my meaning. Then I said, as we didn't like wasting time, I'd also brought in his youngest son and we were going to watch together to see how the kid would stand up to the shock treatment. And they brought him into the room. I just had time to say, we're going to take off your shirt and trousers, young man, like on the beach, we're going to show your Dad a trick, and the guy said he'd talk. And straight off, he began to spill the beans, no problem. We almost had to shut him up! A piece of cake, mon capitaine."

"Well, there you are, Moreau," says the capitaine. "You're becoming an ace psychologist, aren't you? And what then?"

"He gave us a name, mon capitaine. A guy who works at the port. A trade unionist. A storeman, I think. Or an accountant. A commie. A Frenchman, mon capitaine."

"They're all Frenchmen, Moreau."

"Yes, mon capitaine. You know what I mean."

"Yes, Moreau. I know what you mean. Good. You go and fetch him for me. And when he's here, call me."

"At once, mon capitaine."

In the corridor the little boy gets up and starts running. His father has just emerged from the interrogation room between two *harkis*. He is a man of forty-five, tall and wiry. His frizzy hair is almost entirely grey. He bends down to pick up the child in his arms. He hugs him to himself with all his might and throws Capitaine Degorce a long look, filled with gratitude and despair. His eyes are moist, almost tearful, like those of an old man. His lips tremble.

(*There's no harm in this. It's how things ought to go all the time.*)

"I'll come with you as far as the car, Moreau. I've not been out at all today. I need a breath of air."

The sun is shining and it is very hot now. The sky is still an indeterminate, ugly colour, a pale milky blue that reminds Capitaine Degorce of the devout pictures on the backs of which his mother used to write greetings for his birthday or the new year: the child Jesus would be depicted there, pale and podgy, in a pose of vague solemnity, on his mother's knee, or the martyrdom of obscure saints, being lashed, cut up or boiled alive, their mouths open to emit cries that looked like moans of ecstasy, while in the background angels sounded trumpets in the same pasteboard sky. Capitaine Degorce has never told his mother how embarrassing he found these naive depictions, how little they matched the nature of his faith. He could not help detecting in them something stale and corrupted which he now perceives in the perverseness of the Algerian sky. To the south huge yellow and dark brown clouds are gathering on the horizon. Capitaine Degorce's skin is damp. He goes indoors to wash his hands and rinse his face with cold water. He wants to go back and see Tahar, to sit down facing him in the reassuringly dim light of the cell. He returns to his office where the morning papers have been left. Tahar is on the front page, beneath unanimously triumphant headlines. Capitaine Degorce lacks the courage to read the reports, all that clotted, sterile prose. He fiddles vaguely with his letters again and glances up at the top of the organization chart. The photograph of Tahar ought to be marked with a red cross, but he does not want to do it. A foolish superstition. He will be decorated or promoted for having arrested him, that is certain, and the notion is suddenly intolerable to him.

(*Time will pass, thank God.*)

Time will pass. He will leave El-Biar. He will leave Algeria. He will return to Piana for another holiday and rediscover pure air again, rediscover the joy of speaking spontaneously, once he has embraced his wife, kissed his children's brows, they will come to life once again and rediscover their places in his heart.

(*But how will I be able to embrace them?*)

He gets up and marks the red cross. Soon the organization chart will be completely covered in red crosses and he will be a commandant. He thinks about this with indifference now. The future is just as unreal as the world that surrounds him. In the photograph on the organization chart Tahar looks sad and resigned. On the front pages of the newspapers all this sadness has disappeared. He smiles politely, as if the photographers thronging around him were worthy of his consideration and courtesy. At his side the colonel is smiling too, a ghastly complacent smile: for all the world as if the two of them were about to go out to dinner together. And Capitaine Degorce suddenly realizes that it is these photos that have saved Tahar's life. The previous day the colonel had been unable to resist his impulse to summon the press so he could strut before them like a peacock, he arranged this on his own initiative with no thought of anything other than satisfying his own vanity and this initiative has not found favour in high places because now that Tahar has been in the limelight he can no longer disappear.

(Thank goodness for that idiot.)

The generals must have been livid, including Salan himself, and doubtless the resident minister, they must have rung Paris and ordered the colonel to find a solution, but there is no solution, it is too late and the colonel is reduced to simmering in his own helplessness, regretting that things had not turned out differently. Capitaine Degorce can hear his exasperated voice on the telephone, he remembers his repellent insinuations and feels humiliated that he should be supposed capable of carrying out such foul tasks without turning a hair, as if he were a hitman, a performer of dirty jobs and not a French officer, and rage overwhelms him to the point that he almost telephones the colonel to hurl abuse at him.

(What have you made of me, my God, what have you made of me?)

But nothing lasts. His most powerful emotions cannot sustain their intensity for long, they become pallid and tepid and are all blended together into a vague feeling of desperate weariness that does not leave him. Everything is false and hollow. How could he have failed to understand at once what the colonel meant? Who's the idiot now? There must be icy, reptilian blood flowing in his veins. His thoughts are slow, bogged down, constantly faltering. They no longer interest him.

(What have you made of me, my God, what have you made of me?)

And the voice says "my God" well enough, but he does not know to whom this question is addressed.

*

Robert Clément. Twenty-four. Accountant in a shipping company. Came to Algeria in 1954. A slightly built young man with a patchy moustache that makes his face look even more youthful. He sits on the chair with his back very straight and stares at Capitaine Degorce and Adjudant-chef Moreau with open disdain. His shirt is soaked in sweat under the arms.

(The big moment in his life.)

There is a protracted silence and when Capitaine Degorce considers it has lasted long enough he asks cheerfully: "So, are you a communist?"

"That's no concern of yours," the young man replies, "but yes, I'm a communist. Is that a crime now?"

"Oh no, not at all!" the capitaine exclaims, smiling and adds with conviction, leaning towards Clément: "I've nothing against communists, you know. Nothing at all. Indeed quite the contrary. I owe my life to a communist, just imagine. It's true! If you stay with us for long enough I may have the chance to tell you all about it. Raymond Blumers. Does that mean anything to you? In the Resistance."

(Truth. Lies.)

Clément shakes his head. "No."

"No?" Capitaine Degorce repeats sadly.

"No. And I couldn't care less about it."

"Mon capitaine," suggests Adjudant-chef Moreau. "Maybe if I tickled him in the chops a couple of times it would improve the comrade's manners."

"No, Moreau, no," says the capitaine. "Monsieur Clément is

vexed and I expect he has reasons for this. We can make the effort to understand his little emotional fluctuations. Because he knows very well that being a communist is not a crime. But assisting the rebellion is a different matter. That's more than a crime. It's treason. What do you think about that, Monsieur Clément? Do you think 'treason' is the right word or can you perhaps convince us that it's an exaggeration?"

"I've betrayed no-one," says Clément. "And you have no right to detain me for my ideas. I demand that you release me."

Moreau gives a loud guffaw. Capitaine Degorce adopts a contrite expression.

"I'm afraid you don't understand the situation. There is no right. There is only you, locked up here with us. For as long as we deem necessary. Or for as long as I choose. I could keep you here until the Last Judgement – oh, excuse me – until the Revolution comes, you see, I'm flexible. We don't have to account to anyone. And for as long as you don't talk, believe me, you won't leave here."

The capitaine turns to Moreau.

"We'll give our young friend some time to think about all that."

The adjudant-chef touches Clément's moustache and pulls a face.

"So that's your way of going into mourning for Comrade Stalin, is it? Well it makes you look like an idiot, my lad. You look like a right idiot."

"Just leave him to stew for a bit," says Capitaine Degorce, once the door is closed. "And then you can come back and turn up the heat. But don't lay a finger on him. Scare the living daylights out of him. But don't lay a finger on him. I don't want him to be able to say anything at all about us when he gets out of here. Understood, Moreau?"

"Yes, mon capitaine."

*

"I'm getting a meal brought to us. I've had nothing to eat all day."

Tahar is still in his socks. His shoes have been placed in a corner, slippers of plaited leather. Capitaine Degorce gives them a quick satisfied glance before plunging into gloom as he recognizes in this the tangible and ludicrous symbol of his own power. He has the power to make a pair of shoes appear or disappear, to decide who shall remain naked and for how long, he can give orders for day and night to be excluded from the cells, he is the master of water and fire, the master torturer, he controls a vast, complicated machine, full of tubes, electric wires, buzzing sounds and flesh, a machine which is almost alive. He supplies it constantly with the organic fuel its insatiable greed demands. He makes it function, but it rules his existence and against it he can do nothing. He has always despised power, the immeasurable powerlessness its exercise conceals, and he has never felt so powerless. A soldier brings two plates and Tahar eats heartily.

"You know," Capitaine Degorce finally remarks, "I don't get the impression your arrest has really pleased my superiors."

"Of course," agrees Tahar.

"Why of course?"

Tahar finishes the contents of his plate and wipes his mouth.

"In chess, I believe, there are situations where in the middle of the game one of the players understands that he can no longer win. Any possible move, any move at all, whatever he does, will only make his position more difficult, you understand. Every choice is a bad choice. And the player knows this but has to continue the game. Perhaps, if he is skilled, he can make it last a little longer, but nothing decisive can happen now. This is your situation, even if you yourself are not aware of it. Not arresting me is bad. Arresting me may be worse. There are only bad choices. For us, capitaine, the opposite is true. If we win here, that's good. If we lose, if you arrest everybody, it's still good. A martyr is a thousand times more useful than a fighter. That's why you will never see victory. You will make a good move or two and on account of these good moves . . ." Tahar shrugs fatalistically: "You will end by losing. If God wills!" he concludes with a smile.

(*So that's it. A fanatic. Cold and calculating. A fanatic's calm indifference. That's all it is.*)

The disappointment is not painful, however. It makes everything easier to bear, starting with himself. Capitaine Degorce does not even feel as if he has been duped. He does not regret the time spent here, nor having naively allowed himself to make regrettable admissions. It makes no difference now. Everything is perfect, inoffensive and smooth.

"I don't play chess," says Capitaine Degorce, getting up. "I'll leave you now."

"I'm very sorry for you," Tahar murmurs.

Capitaine Degorce turns abruptly to face him.

"Pardon?" he says frostily. "I beg your pardon?"

Tahar is leaning forward, his hands clasped, and looks at him with sad eyes. The capitaine feels the painful burning of his compassion, he would like to be angry, summon up stinging words and walk out without looking back, but is incapable of this. He stands there at a loss, his certainties brusquely reduced to ashes.

"You need faith, capitaine, it's a vital need, I believe," says Tahar, "and you have lost faith . . . Please, sit down for a moment more . . ."

And Capitaine Degorce sits down.

". . . You have lost faith and you cannot recover it because everything you are fighting for no longer exists. And I'm very sorry for you."

"What do you know about it?" asks the capitaine in a toneless voice.

"There are so many things that have to be renounced," Tahar says sadly, leaning forward even more, "so many things, you think I don't know? I know and so do you, and there are some men who manage it very well, it's very easy for them. But someone like you . . . How could you manage it without a little faith? It's impossible, quite impossible . . ."

Capitaine Degorce gently shakes his head.

"Faith?" he asks. "Do you think faith can justify what you've done? In Philippeville? At the Milk Bar? At El-Halia?"

He intended his question to be ironic and is amazed that it does not sound it at all. "Or, indeed, what I'm doing, here?" he asks again.

"Oh no!" replies Tahar. "Faith justifies nothing . . . That's not its role, no . . . Besides, what use are justifications?"

Capitaine Degorce does not reply.

"I should like to smoke," says Tahar and the capitaine lights two cigarettes. Tahar settles back against the wall and smokes with visible pleasure.

"Have you ever been out into the *bled*, the interior, capitaine?" he asks after a moment.

"Yes, I've been there," Capitaine Degorce replies, "and I can see what you're driving at. I can see very well. I'm not saying everything is as it should be. I know there are things . . . injustices . . . But there are other ways. And when peace is restored, you'll see . . . We can put things right . . ."

He is dismayed to realize how little he believes in what he is saying. Words have become heavy again, indigestible, dirty.

"It's true, capitaine," says Tahar with a smile. "That's precisely how it will happen. We will put things right. But not you."

He suppresses a yawn and carefully stubs out his cigarette.

"What's the weather outside?" he asks.

"It's a fine day," Capitaine Degorce says. "And hot."

"A fine day," repeats Tahar.

"Would you like to have some air for a while?" Capitaine Degorce asks. "Have a walk in the courtyard? I could, if you like, if you'll give me your word . . ."

"I cannot give you any word." Tahar cuts him off. "Besides it's simpler if I stay here. It's much simpler like this."

"As you wish."

They remain silent. Tahar closes his eyes. Capitaine Degorce has hardly touched his meal. The congealed food left on his plate rather disgusts him. He ought to summon a soldier to clear away. He ought to smoke less. He would like to continue the discussion, but he says nothing. The war bores him now. He would like to ask Tahar to talk about his family, he would like to talk about his own, tell him how he loved mathematics more than anything and it was only after the war that he decided to embark on a military career. He would like to be able to forget the handcuffs, the walls of the cell, the barricaded city. Tahar opens his eyes and leans towards him once more.

"Above all, capitaine," he says, with much warmth and conviction, "whatever you do, don't believe you're to be pitied, I urge you. You're not to be pitied. Do you know that?"

"I don't complain about anything."

"That's good. Because you're not to be pitied. And neither am I."

*

A terrible south wind has arisen from the Sahara, an apocalyptic wind, twisting the tops of the palm trees, whirling along the empty avenues and it has spread a yellow light saturated with dust and sand over the city. All other colours have disappeared. The white of the great Haussmann-style apartment buildings that line the streets, has become ochre and the blue cast iron work seems to be forged in dark amber. Sergent Febvay and one of the soldiers are staring curiously out of the window.

"Alright, lads, this is not a weather station," growls Adjudant-chef Moreau.

"Well, Moreau," asks Capitaine Degorce, "is he showing sense, that fellow?"

On hearing his voice Febvay turns round and salutes. He has a bruise on his left cheekbone. Not as large as the capitaine would have liked. But this does nothing for him. He observes Febvay's contrite face, his look of a child caught out in wrongdoing, and no longer feels any anger towards him. Rather a schoolmaster's secret sympathy for an unruly dunce.

"Mon capitaine," begins Febvay, "I just wanted to say . . ."

Capitaine Degorce makes a brief hand gesture.

"Right, Febvay. Not another word about it. Not another word. Do your job and watch your step. Well?" the capitaine asks again, turning to Moreau.

"Nothing, mon capitaine," says Moreau. "Nothing at all. He's acting high and mighty. He's as good as telling us to fuck off. He's spouting a whole rigmarole about freedom of thought and the emancipation of oppressed peoples. A whole lot of bollocks like that. A real variety act."

"We're in no hurry," says Capitaine Degorce. "I'm sure he won't hold out."

"With your permission, mon capitaine," remarks Moreau. "He'll hold out even less if we apply a little current to his goolies, not very much, mind you. This one's all mouth, nothing more . . ."

"Not like the Kabylian," says Febvay.

"Oh, the Kabylian," says one of the soldiers. "Now he had balls, that one!"

A brief discussion follows concerning the respective merits of various suspects under interrogation in which it is unanimously agreed that the courage and endurance of Abdelkrim Ait Kaci were exceptional and Moreau gives great admiring nods of his chin with a look in his eyes akin to nostalgia. "A man of courage, yes . . ." agrees Capitaine Degorce and he is appalled to realize that he, too, is beginning to find conversations of this type irresistibly fascinating.

(*Oh, the poverty of our souls!*)

Men's minds are capable of encompassing so many marvellously diverse things. But from those first days at Buchenwald, Capitaine Degorce remembers, they lose their attraction and quite simply cease to exist, beginning with the most elevated, the most worthy of respect, until, in the end, the simplest abstract thought becomes impossible. If the truth be told there is no thought at all and all that is left in the brutalized and shrunken mind are the typical concerns of an incredibly primitive life form, a blind, patient and obstinate one – a bacterium imprisoned in an ageless glacier, a larva in the darkness. Tirelessly you contemplate, your eyes shining with desire and respect, the voluptuous spectacle of a mouth methodically chewing a piece of bread. Three bodies hang from the gibbet, other condemned men await their turn, and you can think about nothing other than the moment when you will take refuge in the huts from the cold wind of autumn 1944 which sweeps the courtyard, causing the corpses to revolve at the ends of their ropes. The God you stubbornly pray to is now no more than a tyrannical and barbaric idol from which you no longer expect anything further than escaping a little bit more from his boundless and unreasonable anger. All the resources of the brain have become wholly condensed into a kind of instinctive and servile cunning, and all that remains of your former feelings are abrupt surges of irrational emotion, like the arbitrary affection with which Raymond Blumers, a veteran of the Spanish Civil War, suddenly surrounded André Degorce, old Blumers, who derided his crossing himself and his prayers and called him "the little priest", but who used all his mysterious influence so that André's name would appear on the list for the *Arbeitstatistik* squad, snatching him, as if by magic, from the hard labour that was gradually killing him and sending him to do accounting in an office, and now every evening, as he ate his soup, André threw Blumers glances filled with animal gratitude, but he did not shed a tear when he witnessed his hanging in February 1945, once more rooted to the spot, grotesquely standing to attention, on the vast parade ground, any more than he wept when he thought about his parents or about Lézieux, or about what life might hold in store, because in what life has become there is no longer any room for pure sorrow. And this, too, is criminal – but it is how life protects and perpetuates itself, by making itself blind and deaf. It has taken Capitaine Degorce such a long time to understand that he was not guilty of any crime and when the Americans forced the people of Weimar to visit the camp, he was the one who lowered his eyes in shame in front of them. And now something similar has happened once again, just here, on the other side of this sombre mirror, for himself and for all the men under his command, something he cannot pardon, even if he no longer lowers his eyes in front of anyone.

(*My God, what have you made of me?*)

"I'm going to my office."

"Very good, mon capitaine."

Febvay smiles at him and he smiles back.

(*These are the outer limits of the world. Interrogation rooms. Endless cells and corridors. This appalling yellow sky. Lost bodies. Lost souls. Unbearable nakedness.*)

It is all they have in common: forecasts and assessments of the resistance of bodies, as if their work did not consist in gathering intelligence at all but in arranging a series of tests, designed to throw light on some hidden, essential, primitive factor, the unique source of all value. They are researchers, specialists in a subtle form of analysis, obsessive visionaries, and the mystery it is given to them to contemplate today, as a reward for their zeal and devotion, has burned their eyes. Night has fallen over all they once loved and they have forgotten it, possibly for ever. The image comes back to Capitaine Degorce of the faceless figure leaning over him at the Gestapo post at Besançon, he can hear the panting breath, he catches a shifty glance at his bruised body, the corner of the mouth twitches with greed and disgust and he knows that he understands this man as intimately as if he had become a part of himself. He understands Moreau, he understands Febvay and the humblest of his soldiers without having to exchange a single word with them. They have undergone the same metamorphosis and become brothers. The circumstances of their past lives count for nothing, any more than the nausea which the revelation of this kinship provokes in him. He no longer has any other family and the people who write to him every day are strangers. The ties that bound him to his parents, to Jeanne-Marie and the children, have vanished, leaving behind, like an absurd imprint, only a certain number of habits and automatic thoughts which it is impossible to be rid of, but which no longer signify anything. Perhaps those ties themselves only ever existed in the form of inconsistent notions or conventions, it is impossible to remember and Capitaine Degorce has the feeling that he has been transported so far away he will never return. He ought to have the courage to cease replying to the letters still lying there on the desk, filled with incomprehensible phrases and sentiments.

"... a little springtime snowfall, that came from the Jura, which has frozen our bones to the marrow ..."

"... and everyone is so proud of you, André: Jean-Baptiste, although he is enjoying his retirement, is almost sorry he can no longer ..."

"... and you know, dear brother-in-law, how grateful I am to you for taking care of Jacques, for whom you will be the model and the father he deserves, while I am nothing but ..."

It would have been better for Claudie not to have been born and for Jeanne-Marie's first husband not to have died. Perhaps she still thinks of him with longing when she walks past the photograph on the living-room wall. Capitaine Degorce is resigned to never matching up to this first love, of which he knows nothing. He is well aware that Jeanne-Marie always gave herself to him with more compassion than desire and for the first time he feels a painful bitterness about this.

(It's true, everything I'm fighting for no longer exists.)

But in reality the thoughts oppressing him carry no weight and the lightest breeze disperses them. He is being unjust towards himself and even more unjust towards those who love him. It is not true, he has not distanced himself from them and what he is fighting for is still alive, he is carrying out a mission, an extremely painful and taxing one, but indispensable in order to put a final end to the terrorist attacks. No other method of action is conceivable and he is not called upon to justify himself. Only a coward and a traitor like Général de Bollardière can put his own sentiments before the needs of the common good. He is not a coward. Later on he will explain this to Jeanne-Marie. For the moment he needs to concentrate and not to forget this fact. He needs to clarify his mind once and for all and put an end to these exhausting and pointless mood swings. He reads the letter from his parents attentively and promises to write them a good, long reply.

*

He is in the middle of staring at a blank sheet, pen in hand when the ringing of the telephone rescues him. The colonel's voice is amazingly soft and controlled.

"We're handing Hadj Nacer over to the law, Degorce. He's being sent to Paris. He'll have to find a way to save his own head. Or else let them cut it off. We've done more than play our part, it seems to me."

"Very good, sir. Where should I take him? And when?"

"You, Degorce, will not be taking him anywhere. Your role stops here. And, by the way, I am to pass on to you the heartiest congratulations from . . ."

His tone is frank and warm now, but Capitaine Degorce no longer hears him.

"Sir," he interrupts. "What does that mean, my role stops here? What arrangements are envisaged?"

"Lieutenant Andreani will come to collect Hadj Nacer tonight. Just Hadj Nacer, and he will take charge of him until his transfer to metropolitan France tomorrow during the day."

"Sir," says Capitaine Degorce, trying to master an emotion he cannot explain to himself. "Sir, I don't understand the purpose of proceeding in this way and I request permission to take care of Hadj Nacer up to the end."

"No," says the colonel.

"Sir," insists Capitaine Degorce, "he's my prisoner. Andreani has nothing to do with this, and I insist . . ."

"Not another word, dammit!" explodes the colonel. "Your prisoner! *Your* prisoner? Who do you think you are, in God's name? You're an officer, dammit! An officer in the French Army, not a bandit chieftain. And you have superior officers, remember. Superior officers who make decisions without needing your advice, is that clear?"

"Sir, I don't understand the point of involving Lieutenant . . ."

"Listen, Degorce," says the colonel with a sigh. "My God, frankly,

I'm being very patient with you. There may well be matters you are not aware of. Who knows, security considerations, for example . . ."

"Sir, the prisoner is perfectly secure here and . . ."

"That's enough!" roars the colonel. "Andreani will come tonight and that's all there is to it! I'm fed up to the back teeth with your idiocies."

And he hangs up.

*

He cannot understand what it is that distresses him to this extent. Regret at having wasted his time trying to write impossible words instead of spending it with Tahar or the prospect of handing him over to Andreani. He puts away the writing paper and paces round his office, smoking. He would like to be able to do something, but he does not know what to do. He calls Moreau and informs him of the decisions made by the general staff.

"Fine," says Moreau.

"Now this is what we're going to do," says Capitaine Degorce. "Pick five men for me and keep them in readiness. And when Andreani arrives and we take Hadj Nacer to him they will pay him the full military compliments."

"Military compliments, mon capitaine?"

"Do you have a problem with that? Does it shock you? Please speak freely."

Moreau shrugs.

"Listen," Capitaine Degorce, goes on. "We have to be able to show respect to worthy enemies. This is something that does honour to us. Do you understand? It's important."

"Fine, mon capitaine."

"Tarik Hadj Nacer is a worthy enemy, Moreau. Truly worthy."

"Very good, mon capitaine, I'll see to it," says Moreau, doing an about-turn.

The capitaine remains sitting on the edge of his desk for a moment, then goes out into the corridor.

"Moreau! Come back here for a moment. I haven't finished."

"Yes, mon capitaine?"

"Look here, Moreau, there's something you ought to know. This is my own initiative. It's quite personal on my part. I've not told anyone about it. I don't have anyone's authorization and I'm not sure I would have been able to get it. So there you are, I'm not ordering you to do this, Moreau. If you have a problem with it I'll ask someone else to see to it. You must feel totally free. I should welcome your support, but I shall not hold it against you if you want to opt out. You have my word. I'll find someone else. There you are. You decide."

"What you're doing has my full support, mon capitaine," Moreau replies at once. "That's what I think. I'll see to it. I'll be glad to see to it. Thank you for taking me into your confidence, mon capitaine."

(*My family.*)

"It is I who thank you, adjudant-chef," murmurs Capitaine Degorce, shaking his hand. "Thank you."

He feels completely at ease, cleansed and relieved. He has succeeded in arranging for matters to turn out honourably. He perceives the future in glowing colours. Just a few more weeks and it will all be over. He will have done his duty and will know that it was not in vain. Pointless questions will no longer arise. Tahar will have the fair trial he deserves and one day soon, a day which will finally dawn, everything will be behind them and they will no longer be enemies. He opens the door of the cell in good spirits. Tahar looks up at him.

"It's all arranged," Capitaine Degorce announces as he sits down. "They'll come to collect you tonight and tomorrow you'll be handed over to stand trial in France."

"Good," says Tahar. "Tomorrow. And tonight, where will I spend tonight?"

"Away from here," Capitaine Degorce replies. "In the charge of the officer I am to hand you over to, I suppose. At Saint-Eugène."

Tahar closes his eyes.

"Tomorrow's Friday," he whispers. "I'm fortunate."

"What do you mean?" asks Capitaine Degorce and the anxiety he thought was gone burns his chest again.

Tahar smiles sadly.

"It doesn't matter."

Capitaine Degorce is sitting less than six feet away from him, but he feels as if an infinite distance lay between them and it has always been thus. The hearts of men are such a mystery. This one's heart is an even greater one. The capitaine would like to be able to wrest Tahar out of his solitude and draw him towards him, if only for moment, and he looks at him with an almost imploring goodwill.

(One day this war will be over and you and I will once again sit face to face in full sunlight, and we shall be able to talk, then, we shall be able to tell one another all that we have not had time to say here.)

"One day this war will be over, you'll see," says Capitaine Degorce.

"I know, capitaine," says Tahar.

He has not re-opened his eyes. His features have slowly subsided and he looks very old. Shadows obscure his face where deep lines, that can be guessed at already, will form, lying in wait at the corners of his eyes, on his brow, in the hollows of his cheeks. And little by little the shadows fade away, the bitter line of the mouth slowly becomes a smile, cracks appear in the mask of old age and it silently breaks up. The eyes open, but the light shining in them remains indecipherable. All the things Capitaine Degorce would like to say seem to him empty and inappropriate.

"I shall come to fetch you," he simply says before leaving the cell.

He goes out into the street to smoke a cigarette. The wind has dropped and a vast sun is setting slowly over the city. Grains of sand cling to the windows and the wire mesh. The air is laden with dust and humidity. Capitaine Degorce wonders how anyone can become attached to this city. If it possesses a secret charm, he finds it impossible to detect. He will leave it with no regrets. In the interrogation room Febvay sits on a table, eating a large apple, cutting it in pieces with a commando knife, from time to time directing furious glances at Robert Clément, who is handcuffed to a radiator. He spits the pips in his direction.

"Still nothing," notes Capitaine Degorce.

"Nothing at all, mon capitaine."

The capitaine kneels beside Clément.

"The nights here are not very pleasant, you know," he confides. "And the worst of it is that you never get used to them. I've noticed that. Each night is worse than the last. They're wrong to say you can get used to everything. Folk wisdom doesn't amount to much, does it?"

Clément maintains a stubborn silence.

"Well, you'll see for yourself. But it's foolish. And utterly pointless, believe me. Don't bring it upon yourself. Now I'll tell you what's going to happen. Tomorrow, or the day after tomorrow, someone in your family, your mother perhaps, or your fiancée, is going to come here and ask for news of you. And do you know what I'm going to reply? No? I'm going to tell them we released you this afternoon and I'm very surprised she still has no news of you. I shall offer her all my sympathy and ask her not to fail to keep me informed. I shall appear anxious, very anxious. I know my anxiety is particularly contagious. And when she's gone I'll come and describe every detail of the scene to you. I shall leave nothing out, you can be sure of that. You may possibly listen to me with more of your splendid indifference, through pride or stupidity. And then there will be another night and you'll think about all this again. You won't be able to help thinking about it. You'll realize that you no longer exist. You'll think about the distress of your loved ones. They're terrible, night thoughts. I've noticed that as well. I'm very observant. You'll end up seeing things differently. You'll tell me what I want to know, I'm sure of it."

The capitaine studies Clément and leans closer to his ear.

"And if I'm wrong, and being mistaken really annoys me, which for your sake I hope won't be the case, here's what I may do. I'll release you. I'll take you to your work place and take my leave of you very warmly, I promise you. I'll even embrace you and before that my men will have put the word round everywhere, in all the right circles, showering you with praise. They'll talk about your enthusiasm for assisting the army of your beloved country, and the courage with which you have agreed to go under cover, you see. And your release will be followed by a wave of very public arrests. I'll make sure of that. I don't think you'll have time to pack your bags."

Capitaine Degorce gives Clément a couple of friendly pats on the shoulder.

"Do you know what your friends in the F.L.N. do to traitors? I've got some photographs if it interests you."

Clément turns towards the capitaine and spits in his face. Febvay leaps to his feet.

"Leave him, Febvay." Capitaine Degorce restrains him, wiping his face. "Leave him. This means that Monsieur Clément has already begun to think. Lock him up for the night. In solitary."

(*Filthy little shit.*)

*

The sheets of paper are no longer blank. On each one of them he has written the date and "Dear Mother and Father," "My dearest wife, my beloved children", and even, "My dear Marcel". And that is all. It is eleven o'clock and night has fallen. He has forced himself to eat something and sits there, pen in hand, turning his head every time there is the sound of an engine. He picks up the start of the letter intended for Marcel and tosses it into the waste paper basket with the feeling of having effectively solved a part of his problem. "Dear Mother and Father, look after your health, especially you, papa. Everything here is going as well as possible. Your son, André." No point in rereading it. The thing to do is to put it into an envelope as quickly as possible and stop thinking about it. Words will come back. "My dearest wife, my beloved children, an extremely busy day prevents me from writing to you at length and only leaves me time to tell you that all's going well and to send you my fondest love." Outgoing mail. His mind is intact. He is capable of developing complex arguments and taking decisions. He can formulate and understand the givens of a problem, assess the relative importance of intelligence. He knows how to devise plans which call for the elaboration of middle-term and long-term conjectures. But naturally, when it comes to writing a letter to his nearest and dearest, something else is needed, something he has plainly lost. His soul, perhaps, the soul which brings words to life. He has left his soul behind somewhere along the way and he does not know where. Tomorrow he will have to resume this ordeal – writing, writing at least something, and he regrets not having kept copies of his letters, so that he could send them again, unchanged. But, in fact, that is virtually what he has been doing for weeks now. A copy would be quite pointless. He looks at the organization chart. When he has completed it he will be able to retrace his steps and retrieve his soul, wherever he has left it. For the time being what lies within him is a desert.

(*And my thoughts are like graffiti on the walls of an empty room.*)

Everything is silent. It is a fearful hour of the night. The daylight is fled and will not reappear for a long time. It is the hour when Christ's heart was filled with anguish in the darkness of the garden of Gethsemane, the apostles had abandoned him into sleep, leaving him to his appalling solitude, and his heart is the frail heart of a man, terrified at the approach of death. He falls face downwards upon the ground, the leaves of the olive trees shiver in the wind and there is nothing to keep the bitter chalice at bay. It is the hour when the soldiers of the Sanhedrin are arming and the melancholy Procurator of Judaea paces the corridors of his silent palace, endlessly putting off the hour when he goes to bed. For him, too, this night is a night of anguish and he does not know why. He broods on the terrors of childhood and is devastated that they have returned to trouble the austere and serious man he has become. He has a taste of blood in his mouth and his soul is exceeding sorrowful unto death. Capitaine Degorce switches off the light in his office and paces, in his turn, along interminable corridors, he walks slowly, without meeting anyone, and feels as if he were a prisoner in an endless labyrinth. In the end he finds Moreau.

"I'm going to lie down for a while. Wake me when Andreani arrives."

In his room he picks up his Bible and sniffs the pages. The delicious scent of paper and glue calms him. He reads: "Then shall he say also unto them on the left hand, Depart from me, ye cursed, into everlasting fire, prepared for the devil and his angels: for I was an hungred and ye gave me no meat: I was thirsty, and ye gave me no drink: I was a stranger and ye took me not in: naked, and ye clothed me not: sick and in prison and ye visited me not." Capitaine Degorce lies down, fully clothed, on his bed with his eyes open. It is this text that is an endless labyrinth. He gets up again. The corridors, once more, and the door of the cell and finally Tahar, who asks him, straightening up: "Is it time?"

"No," replies Capitaine Degorce. "I have come to wait for it with you, if that does not disturb you. Let me stay with you, please," he says again – and Tahar smiles at him.

I remember you, mon capitaine, and I can still see you in court walking towards the bench without even a glance at the dock where Paul Mattei and I were watching as you passed by. You were wearing all your decorations and the brand-new insignia of a lieutenant-colonel. They may have ended up making you a général, but don't hold it against me, mon capitaine, if I stick with the rank you held as a young man, the only one you owed to your courage and not to your utter servility, a servility so great that even today I may well not have grasped the full extent of it. For I am stubborn, and the love I bore you has left such a deep trace in my heart that I have never been able to abandon the absurd hope of meeting you again, a hope that has been endlessly disappointed, of course, as it was in April 1961, when, right up to the last moment, I believed you would come over to us in support of the generals and l'Algérie française. You were only a commandant then, I had not seen you since the fighting at Wilaya 5, and even though I was already aware of that victory meaning nothing to you and of your being ready to allow yourself to be robbed of it to the benefit of Tahar's friends, who had so little deserved it, I nevertheless believed you would not accept having shed all that blood for nothing, blood that victory alone could make sense of. Yes, mon capitaine, I am stubborn and I refused to see that deep down you were nothing more than a lackey, a faithful servant, grateful to his masters for the baubles with which they reward his base conduct, but you stayed put, you accepted the ignominy imposed on us, without turning a hair, like the other lackeys, our former brothers in arms, of whom we learned that, one after the other, they were defecting, despite all their solemn promises, and Paul Mattei said to me, Horace, it can't end like this. No, mon capitaine, nothing could end like that, in a grotesque, final charade, neither that war, nor our revolt, for we refused to forget our promises, and we kept them, whatever the cost, by renouncing everything that had driven our lives up until then, that cowardly army, the nation of lackeys that had betrayed its own memory and shamefully turned a blind eye as Belkacem and his kin were being taken to the slaughterhouse, as if the blood of these men counted for nothing, and I could not prevent it, but I could keep my promises and show that blood had a price, an exorbitant price, one that had to be paid. At the opening of our trial Paul stood up and asked, of what am I to be absolved? after which he remained silent, but as for me, mon capitaine, I did not honour them with a single word, I left them to the virtue of their selective indignation, refusing to participate in any way in the proceedings of that masquerade, I did not even object when our counsel sought to subpoena you as a witness. Oh, maybe it was not solely on principle, after all, mon capitaine, that I made no objection, maybe I was still expecting something from you, for I am stubborn, or maybe a secret part of me, hidden in the depths of my heart, was overjoyed at the prospect of seeing you again, no-one can say, and I listened to you giving your evidence to the court, I heard you speaking in conventional terms about our exemplary conduct in Indochina, about the difficulties of service in Algeria and the exceptionally tragic circumstances that might perhaps mitigate the heinousness of our treason, and I was stunned for, except at the moment when you murmured some inept phrase or other about the difficulty of protecting one's soul during that cruel war, you appeared to be reciting a prepared text, you stared rigidly in front of you, I clearly remember, and it was so evident that you were only there out of a sense of duty, our actions inspired so manifest a revulsion in you, that it may well have been your evidence that was the deciding factor in our being condemned to death. No, mon capitaine, I should not be surprised to learn it, but I do not hold it against you, death has been no stranger to me for a long time, as you well know, and it was the prospect of going on living in this fragile, ancient world, that seemed unfamiliar, almost daunting to me then, perhaps I was never able to do justice to life, something my little seminarist already used to deplore in the letters he wrote to me from the slopes of the Djurdjura mountains before an unknown F.L.N. zone chieftain decided to have him executed. Once calm was restored in the city, when our work at the villa in Saint-Eugène was finished, I did everything I could to avoid him being given a combat posting, even though he had made known his wish to remain with me, but he had done enough, it had not been his choice and he deserved peace. It is, of course, still painful to me that, in seeking to grant him peace, I set him on a course towards those who would murder him, but there were so many murderers about that they doubtless awaited him at the end of any one of the paths that might have taken him far away from the village in Kabylia where he was posted as a teacher. After three months I received his first letter, I clearly remember, this was probably the time it had taken him to emerge from the devastation the villa in Saint-Eugène had buried him in and he felt reborn, he wrote that he thought of me often, and that he would have liked me to be able to come and spend a few days with him, so as to understand what life could be, despite the poverty, despite the war, indeed the war seemed to be so far away, he went on to write, that he quite often left his M.A.T.49 rifle behind in the corner of the classroom where he had set it down that morning, and the children would come running after him to hand him back his gun as he was already walking back to his base, with his hands in his pockets, smiling at the sunset, as if he had finally become a care-free child like the others, and that is how I still picture him today. He thanked me for having given him this chance and commiserated with me, he said he was certain that it would one day be granted to me, too, to be reborn and that he would never go back to metropolitan France, even when the war was over, he would remain there with his children, he would be teaching them to write their names in fine rounded script, teach them to sing counting rhymes, to do the conga amid gleeful shouts along the lanes of the village and to twist together the endless supply of plastic scoubidou threads that his mother used to send him by post, and which the little girls would attach to their multicoloured necklaces amid laughter, he wrote me their names, but these have slipped my memory, Djeyda, Ghozlene, Dihya, and he repeated that he would never abandon them, he would continue to watch them marvelling at being photographed, as they sat on the school courtyard wall, the vivid colours of their best dresses glowing in the summer light, and he would never walk away from the smiles that both broke his heart and filled him with a love of life so indomitable that not even the memories of suffering and death that some-times kept him awake at night could tarnish its radiance. He had, of course, lost his faith in God, but the new faith that inspired him seemed enduring and he had no regrets. His pupils' parents sometimes invited him to eat a modest vegetable couscous with them, or, on feast days, a roast boar, the unclean portion of which had been scrupulously removed, cursed and thrown into the fire, he would get back to the base later and later, with an ever more carefree tread and it was on his return from one of these meals, one night in 1959, that he got himself killed. The sous-lieutenant in command of the base only noticed his absence the following day and they found his mutilated body beside the road. His M.A.T.49 had vanished. If I had been in command of that base, mon capitaine, I should have arrested the whole of the family who had invited him to dinner, knowing he would be returning alone in the darkness, I should have had their hovel burned, but I did not even suggest this to that idiot of a sous-lieutenant and, in memory of my little seminarist, I settled for believing that all the smiles that had lit up his last weeks had been pure and sincere and I simply asked to be allowed to write the letter myself that had to be sent to his parents. This was contrary to normal practice, but the sous-lieutenant agreed at once – in fact I was relieving him of an unwelcome chore, all he would have been capable of doing would be stringing out the same set phrases which you yourself used at my trial, mon capitaine, exemplary conduct, tragic circumstances, all that nonsense, and his indifference would have sullied my memory of that boy, which mattered so much to me, yes, it mattered to me, and it was from you, mon capitaine, that I learned the need to employ the convoluted paths of untruth so as to preserve the memory of the dead and the essential truth of them, something infinitely more precious than the bald truth of facts. I gathered up his personal effects, letters, a little vocabulary in which he had begun noting words in Kabylian and their meanings, the black Christ wrapped in old newspaper and dozens of photographs he had taken in the village. I addressed the letter to his mother, I told her about the great affection I had for her son, who had served under me for a number of months, during the course of which I had come to appreciate his character and his unswerving moral rectitude, I spoke of the extremely important secretarial work he had carried out for me, but it was only in Kabylia, I wrote, that the mission entrusted to him had been in accord with his deepest aspirations and I assured her that he was happy, so happy that, even while he was aware of the threat that hung over him, he had not wanted to leave, and that perhaps she might find in this some comfort for her grief, I wrote that his death had been quick, that he had not suffered, I gave her my word for this, mon capitaine, I knew his body would be returned to her in a sealed coffin and she would never know what they had made him suffer that night and I wrote that all the children who had become his own were inconsolable, they would never forget him, they would join her in mourning her son, in that village she did not know on the slopes of the Djurdjura mountain range and this, at least, might be true. I finished by offering to visit her, if she wished, on my return to metropolitan France, but, of course, I never had the opportunity to do this, and I packed up all my little seminarist's belongings, apart from the photograph of the little girls in the school courtyard, Massiva, Leïla and Thiziri, which I kept, as I had the right to do, since it was for me he had taken it, for me alone, and still today, when I look at it, I remember him, I remember him clearly, but I think of you too, my brother, mon capitaine, every time I meet those solemn eyes and smiles which it is forbidden to you, and to me, to fathom. I sent off the parcel and the letter and went back to Wilaya 5, where Colonel Lotfi's *katiba* units were raiding our command posts before taking refuge beyond the frontier with Morocco. You ought to have been relieved at once more encountering war as you had always known it, mon capitaine, out in the open, against armed enemies who had finally hauled you out from the damp cellars of El-Biar, but one only needed to look at you for a moment to sense that you were not. Perhaps you had grasped that nothing could halt what had once been begun, and that even here, on the threshold of the Sahara, the only thing that mattered was obtaining intelligence. When one of our patrols was massacred near a village to the south of Béchar, I went into the village with my men where there were children crouched down chewing cat-mint with closed eyes, from time to time wiping away with their cuffs the green saliva that ran down their chins, a large dog with pointed ears, covered in flies, hung from the branch of a stunted tree, I clearly remember. I had all the villagers assembled and, in front of them all I fired a bullet into the head of the village headman, he fell on his side, his scarf unwound on the sand, a woman let out a cry, but the children did not stir, and I asked Belkacem to translate what I told the villagers. I told them they must give up hope of living, I told them they were all going to die and they had no choice between life and death, the only choice they had was at whose hand death came, at mine or that of the rebellion, and I told them I would return every time they gave intelligence to the F.L.N. and not me, I would return every time they gave food to one of the rebels, every time they gave him a drink of water from their well, even a single drop, I would return, they would learn to know me and when they knew me, the only thing they would wish would be for death not to come to them from me. Did I tell you how I obtained the intelligence that enabled us to set that ambush between Taghit and Béhar in 1960? Did I tell you, mon capitaine? I do not think so, but I had no need to tell you, is that not so, for you knew very well, even if you preferred not to be told. It was night. The crescent moon was shining in a starry sky and just beside the long desert road a little dromedary was being suckled by its mother, on trembling, spindly legs. You had the machine guns set up just at the top of a slope and when the men of the *katiba* appeared you gave the command to open fire. The group under my command caught them from the rear as they tried to escape and we took about ten prisoners. I asked them who their officer was, they pointed to a corpse and I made them kneel beside the road. They did not beg, they did not ask questions. No doubt they knew this was the best thing that could happen to them. They fell forward, face downwards in the sand. I heard the little dromedary uttering piteous cries. Its mother had been hit by a burst of gunfire and it was straining towards the great motionless body, trying to reach the teats so as to go on sucking, but it could not manage to do so and it raised its long neck towards the moon, squealing. I had it shot as well. I did not want to leave it to starve to death. When I caught up with you, you asked me how many prisoners we had and I replied that we had no prisoners. I added that we needed the officer's body and you dismissed me with a gesture, looking the other way, as if the only thing that mattered to you was to leave me in no doubt of your contempt. But the truth is that it was I who held you in contempt, mon capitaine, that night more than ever. The next day I went back to the village with the body of the A.L.N. officer, I threw it down at the centre of the village in front of the assembled villagers and told them that the person who had threatened them was dead, and all his men with him, but that I was alive and that only living people were to be feared. They went up to the body, they looked at his face and I swear to you, mon capitaine, that for a brief moment, despite their terror and despair, I sensed their gratitude. I needed their terror and despair, I needed it so that we could achieve the victory of which we were robbed, with your shameful connivance, and for which all those people would have been eternally grateful. I have not forgotten them, you know, and when, years later, outside the Hôtel Saint-George, the taxi driver asked me where my family home was, I named that village to the south of Béchar and he told me he had not realized it was so far away and he could not take me there, not on account of the distance, he had driven longer distances before then, he could have taken me down to the south for several days and would have quoted a price, but on account of the danger. There were a lot of dummy road blocks and he told me that it was just close to that village of mine that a whole wedding party on its way to Taghit had had their throats cut, even the musicians, did I know? and I told him, yes I did know, I knew the road very well where it had happened. It may well have been at the very spot where our machine guns had decimated the *katiba* that they set up their dummy road block, waiting there in their stolen uniforms, and the bride, who was called Zohra, Hayet or Sabah, I simply cannot remember, would have been thinking that this interminable police inspection was going to delay the celebration and the moment of intimacy, and the people went on singing, mon capitaine, they were singing, I love you, Sara, let me live in your heart, and the bride noticed that the policemen were not wearing regulation shoes, the cars slowed down, all eyes were focused on the non-matching shoes and someone screamed while a single voice finished singing, I'd die for you, Sara, and they all knew they were never going to reach Taghit and would never be able to sit down in the shade of the tent erected for them beside the palm grove, at the foot of the earth walls, the bride pressed close to her husband who put his hand on her sterile belly, her old maid's belly, that would never be put to use, and they were made to get out of the cars decorated with white ribbons, the weather was so dry that their blood dried almost instantly and the desert wind set a *darbouka* drum rolling in the dust, it caused the satin robes to billow, sent torn lace flying and carried fine pink grains of sand towards the sea. The taxi driver sadly remarked that there was no end to the way life kept on turning ugly and then began to smile as he pointed out that the sky had darkened, here we have all four seasons on the same day, you see? and I said I know, in one way this is my country too, but he grew sad again and murmured, no, *monsieur*, this is no longer a country, a country of men, it's a slaughterhouse and a prison and what we are is sacrificial lambs, he told me how his daughter of twelve had started wetting her bed every night, she woke herself up crying and was soaked in piss, as if she were not twelve but three, or even two, and the glittering eyes of wolves had come back to lie in wait for her in the darkness, the night was once more filled with wolves and monsters, she could feel their hot breath in the darkness of her nightmares, and she woke up crying out, with the bitter stench of piss in her nostrils, she frightened her little brothers who started crying out as well, and there was nothing to be done, in vain did they cajole her or scold her, tell her she was no longer a child, every night she began again, even smacking her would have been useless and he could not strike his daughter because he loved her and understood her terror, so he would hold her in his arms, all thin and stinking, until she went to sleep again. And he said, you're lucky to have gone away, *monsieur*, but, as you can see, it's started to rain and in an hour's time there will be sun. I made no reply and thought about my little seminarist, I wondered whether his new faith in the power of life would have survived, and for how long, or whether he would finally have realized that children's smiles mean nothing and that it is we, mon capitaine, who are right not to understand this, and I remembered that the paths of untruth sometimes lead to the truth, as you taught me, for I was certain now that, as I had written to his mother, even if he had foreseen his death, he would not have wanted to leave. This is how truth is born from lies, the little seminarist accepted his death and Capitaine Lestrade was a hero, why should they be pitied? But you, mon capitaine, you have had to continue to live, like a lackey, clinging to principles you no longer had the strength to believe in, I realized this that night on the road to Taghit, I remember it clearly, you were staring at the moon as if you were alone in the world and no longer even had the strength to rejoice at your own victories, even your contempt was a sign of weakness. I really must have loved you, not to have understood at that moment that nothing had any importance in your eyes any longer, not even your own petty self, to which you were nevertheless so attached, and if I had understood what you had become, I should never have hoped for your support in 1961 and your pathetic evidence at our trial would not have surprised and hurt me to such an extent, as you have hurt me so many times before, without even being aware of it. It is very hard to resign oneself to living, as I well know, I have known it for such a long time, mon capitaine, and I forbade my counsel to go to the Court of Appeal, I did not want to wait any longer, I did not want to hear any more speeches, I did not want to have to bear my parents' devastated faces in the visitors' room at Fresnes prison any longer, nor Paul Mattei's sister's tears, and I hoped all that would not last, but Salan saved his own skin and I realized they were not going to execute us. The night that followed the announcement of our reprieve Paul tried to kill himself, but they rescued him, they did not even allow him to choose his own death, and when I saw him after he came out of hospital, he said to me, what a farce, Horace, what a farce and what humiliation, I replied, yes, and embraced him. In

1968 we were released and returned home. I had never been back to my village since my return from Indochina, but I still had my house there and a plot in the cemetery. I spent years without speaking a word to the militant communists I had played with during my childhood and they eyed me as if I were the devil. But everything is so weightless, mon capitaine, everything is forgotten so rapidly, hatred turns cold and that coldness fades and we used to get together to play cards in the village bar, in a corner by the fire in winter and under the vine in summer, until we all grew old. I stopped telephoning Paul because we no longer had anything to say to one another, but I never gave up hope of meeting you again, one day, perhaps by chance, I no longer remembered the name of your wife's village and in any case I should not have made the trip there, but I was endlessly expecting to run into you, perhaps shopping in the town, on a street corner, and I knew I should recognize you, for I had already glimpsed the face of the old man you have become, I saw it appear for a moment on that morning in spring 1957, and I remember it clearly. I do not know why I was so eager to see you again, perhaps to settle an old debt which I had allowed to lapse for all these years – for I owe you something, mon capitaine, and have done for a long time, something I no longer want to keep to myself. We had prepared everything, you know, while you were dreaming your daydreams. We had fixed a hook to the ceiling down in the cellar and fastened a rope to it. Whatever you may think, mon capitaine, I do not particularly like causing suffering, I settle for doing what has to be done and doing it well. As we were driving towards Saint-Eugène, Tahar said nothing. Seated between the seminarist and

Belkacem, who was whistling his song, he stared at his manacled hands. When we reached the villa he saw the rope and the chair and did not look surprised. If I could have killed him without his being aware of anything I would have done so, but that was not possible, and I, too, would like to do him justice on this point, mon capitaine, it is true that he was brave, even though this is utterly unimportant. For a moment I was afraid the absurd notion would occur to him of making a speech to us or uttering a historic pronouncement, but he did not do it, he understood the situation and knew it was not the moment to indulge in any kind of ridiculous childishness. But there is one thing he did say, however, yes, he did say something and I owe you the truth. He turned to me and asked, will you pass on a message from me to Capitaine Degorce? and I looked at him and replied no. He was immediately lifted onto the chair to put the rope around his neck, I kicked away the chair and Belkacem put his arms round his waist and hung onto him. The little seminarist remained standing close to the door and turned his head away. Everything was over very quickly. Perhaps I should have heard his message, perhaps I should at least have told you the following morning that he had wanted to say something to you, of which neither you nor I will ever have an inkling, but I could not bring myself to do it, mon capitaine, you treated me like a dog and I had no desire to relieve your suffering, unless, perhaps, it was that I did not want to make you suffer anymore. I could have continued to leave all this buried for ever in the depths of a cellar in Saint-Eugène, but I am stubbornly loyal and the truth is that nothing is buried, I remember everything, I remember it clearly, and have carried everything around with me, the living as well as the dead, which was why I had to go back there, the pitiless land of my childhood having become daily more foreign to me, and I was not lying to the taxi driver when I told him his country was also mine, precisely because it is no longer a country and no country exists for men like me, or like you, mon capitaine. The day before I left I invited the taxi driver to dine with me in the restaurant at the Hôtel Saint-George where, of course, he had never set foot. We drank a *digestif* under the jasmine and he cast uneasy glances at the waiters, as if he were expecting to be thrown out at any moment. The following day, before taking me to the airport which bears the name of one of our enemies, he took me to take tea with him at his home in a public housing unit in Bab-el-Oued. His living room was crowded with plastic cans filled with water, on which his daughter set down the tea and plates piled high with little pastries that came from a *patisserie* where he must have paid a fortune for them. The taxi driver's wife was nursing a crying baby. His daughter sat opposite me and looked at me, smiling, with the same serious and solemn look I had so often encountered in that photograph, taken long ago, one summer morning in Kabylia. I did not ask her her name. When I left she stood up to kiss me. She smelled of eau de cologne. And we drove to the airport, mon capitaine. I knew I would never go back. I shook the taxi driver's hand and I left behind the El-Harrach rubbish tip, the coastal road to Saint-Eugène, the collapsed houses of the Casbah, the wolves' eyes glittering in the darkness and all those children smiling without knowing why, and very far to the south, on the long desert road of our cruel youth, the shade of a nameless bride awaiting her wedding night between Taghit and Béchar.

29 MARCH, 1957: THIRD DAY
John ii, 24–25

His perfect poise is an intolerable insult. The left foot positioned to the rear, resting on the heel, enables the body to pivot gracefully in a single fluid movement. The back is impeccably straight, the shoulder blades project like knives, the back of the neck, close cropped beneath the line of the beret, and Capitaine Degorce would like to empty the magazine of his automatic pistol into this detested neck. But it is too late and he remains seated behind his desk, shaking with humiliation and despair. The previous night there had still been time, but the previous night he was so naive. He had walked slowly alongside Tahar past the soldiers who, on Adjudant-chef Moreau's orders, had just presented arms to him and was so completely filled with the delightful feeling of a duty done that he had not even reacted when Lieutenant Andreani allowed himself to murmur with a sad toss of his head, "Oh! André! My God . . . André . . ." It seemed to him that nothing this man thought could affect him, but that was the moment when he should have taken his pistol from its holster and shot them all down like mad dogs, Horace Andreani, his little weasel of a seminarist and Belkacem. But he did nothing, did not think of it even for a moment, of course, because his eyes were firmly fixed on Tahar as Belkacem thrust him brutally into the car, muttering something in Arabic, and he would have liked Tahar to look back at him one last time and smile at him, but he did not do so and Capitaine Degorce simply mused that this was not how they should have taken their leave of one another, even if they were due to meet again sometime in the full light of day. And now it is forever too late. At the moment when a rope was being put around Tahar's neck Degorce had been enjoying the most peaceful sleep that had been granted him for a long time, nor was he woken by his convulsive death throes. In the morning he drank his coffee and smoked calmly before the open window without knowing that he had become complicit in a crime it would never be possible for him to atone for.

(*You took him from me, Andreani, you took him from me.*)

How could he ever atone for his naivety, his abysmal stupidity, the utter inanity of his optimistic presumptions? He had failed to take on board that brazen impudence now reigns supreme, and a lie no longer needs to clothe itself in the attire of plausibility, it suffices to proclaim, with a complicit wink of an eye, "Tarik Hadj Nacer has committed suicide in his cell," in contempt of all the evidence, and with all the more indifference over being believed because the abject fear that has taken hold of men has finally caused them to love untruth, oh yes, they love it and long for it with all the strength of their slavish souls, but if the most shameless and cool cynicism is also added to this, their adoration knows no bounds and Capitaine Degorce has taken nothing on board, seen nothing, understood nothing: all he is left with is the wretched consolation of not having intended this to happen.

(*But that's the fault, not the excuse. The fault.*)

He would like to telephone the colonel and tell him he is nothing but a base murderer, but he cannot because he, too, is a murderer. He knows one thing for certain: what counts is what he has done, not what he intended and he paces along the corridors, the electric light hurts his eyes, his legs are heavy, and when he finds Moreau he takes his arm and says to him very softly, looking him in the eye: "He's gone, Moreau. They took him from me."

(*I handed him over, it was me.*)

"Now then, mon capitaine," says Moreau, swiftly leading him into the kitchen. "Come in here and sit down. Do you want some water?"

Capitaine Degorce lets himself sink onto a chair.

"You know, don't you? You know what they've done?"

"Yes, mon capitaine. Everyone knows."

Capitaine Degorce passes a hand over his face. He calms down.

"It's not the way, Moreau," he says sadly. "No, it's not the way for us to be fighting a war. Not us."

"This war's a filthy business, mon capitaine," Moreau replies genially. "You know that as well as me."

"Maybe I didn't know."

The adjudant-chef offers him a glass of water. He refuses it with a gesture.

"Order me a vehicle."

*

The driver sets him down in front of Notre-Dame d'Afrique. Throughout the journey he has been imagining the coolness of the basilica, the smells of incense and the damp wood of the confessional and the attentive presence of the priest, on the other side of the grille, but he remains standing on the cathedral steps, his beret in his hand, he sees the figure of Christ on the cross behind the altar, the votive tablets, old ladies nod to him in greeting and he cannot move another inch forward. He has the feeling that if he takes a step forward an invisible hand will drive him away, that the host will burn his mouth like acid. God wants no truck with him. He puts his beret on again and walks further along the square. A light mist hangs over the sea and he hears the sound of the waves breaking against the rocks at Saint-Eugène lower down. All he has failed to achieve can never come to fruition now and he suffers a terrible grief from this. In the distance, in the fiercely barricaded Casbah the muezzin is giving the call to the great Friday prayers, when vast paradises are opened up to the souls of martyrs, and this is what the good fortune Tahar spoke of amounts to, knowing well that he was to die, Capitaine Degorce understands this only now at this moment, and is distressed to think that, knowing it, Tahar had not turned to smile at him one last time. But why should he have smiled at the man who was handing him over to his executioners?

(*I did not know, Lord, I did not know.*)

"Take me back to El-Biar."

The vehicle drives along the sunlit streets and again he pictures himself the night before, sitting close to Tahar, but this time he does not remain unmoving, he gets up without a word, undoes his bonds and takes him by the arm, leads him through the labyrinth of silent corridors to the door open upon a night lit by a slender crescent moon, gently he pushes Tahar towards the brilliance of the moon before closing the door and savouring a new-found peace. He could have done that several hours ago, he could have done it: that is how Pilate, the Procurator of Judaea, must have mused, when the storm of the crucifixion was already rending the Jerusalem sky.

(*And I crave untruth myself, I revel in it. No, oh no, I wouldn't have done it, even if I'd known. I wouldn't have done it. I have the power, and power crushes me, I can do nothing. I have no right to demand explanations. I don't even have a right to regrets.*)

In his office he looks at the photograph of Tahar on the organization chart, he has an impulse to murmur words to excuse himself, but the obscenity of this repels him and his lips remain closed. It is too late. Everything has been said. He picks up his mail. There is only a single letter this morning, from Jeanne-Marie, and he knows he will not be able to open it. He tears it up and tosses the pieces into the waste paper basket. Any word of tenderness would be intolerable. Gilded clouds pass in the sky and he follows them with his eyes through the window. He has the feeling that these are all the happy memories of his life which he has just torn into pieces, as if he had become a man for whom even happy memories are now forbidden and he subsides under the weight of an appalling nostalgia. The rocky pinnacles of Piana tower up in the setting sun and Claudie is playing with Jacques on the terrace of the hotel, but a sickly yellow discolours the sky, even creeping into his memory and he will never again recover its luminous clarity.

(*I am a fog, a sickly sweet rottenness that pervades everything. I am the one corrupting the colours of the creation. I secrete my poison into the world and beauty turns away from me.*)

He used to love beauty so much, with such a fervent love – the sombre beauty of ritual language, the dazzling beauty of mathematics that illuminated his years of study. After two weeks of lessons Charles Lézieux had asked him to take a walk with him after school and told him, while they walked beside the river Doubs, and as if he were almost vexed to have to make this admission, that he was exceptionally talented. And he was. Success cost him no effort, as if he had developed a specific sense, an infallible geometrical intuition which the great majority of his fellow pupils lacked and which enabled him to perceive at once, in a clear light, what the others could only discover after long periods of laborious calculation. For him proofs only confirmed what he had already sensed in advance and he always took the trouble to make them extremely elegant, pure, concise and luminous, for he knew that truth and beauty should be revealed together and that one without the other is worthless. Mathematics opened up an eternal, unchanging, infinite world, without it being necessary to wait for the Day of Judgement. He possessed the key to this world which brought him closer to God and he thought that a life spent exploring it would be perfect. The Grandes Ecoles for engineers did not interest him, to the great satisfaction of Lézieux, who shared his contempt for everything that was basely practical and told him, as they walked side by side, that he was certain he would see him gaining admission to the Ecole Normale Supérieure. But eternity is not sheltered from the world's suffering. The war continued and André Degorce had an increasingly urgent feeling that his blissfully blind existence was a sin. Something evil had spread abroad and this thing, not content with suppressing life, also had to make it shameful and dirty: soon there would be no pathway leading up towards infinite beauty and the souls of men would wither so utterly that they would no longer even be able to regret this. For weeks he had been talking to Lézieux about his desire to make himself useful, but the latter would invariably deflect the conversation to the works of Cantor or the theory of Hilbert spaces, until the day came when he replied that he could give André an opportunity to be useful. The Allies had landed in Normandy and Lézieux doubtless believed his pupil would soon be safe from reprisals. Less than a month later, just before the door to the flat where they were due to meet was broken down, the rapid clatter of footsteps on the staircase froze André's heart and, on his return from Buchenwald, a life dedicated to mathematics had ceased to be conceivable. He had never felt he had a warlike temperament, discipline did not appeal to him and he had no taste for action, but a military career imposed itself upon him as an absolute necessity. The possibility of beauty must be preserved, that was all that mattered, even though he himself must turn away from it and renounce the enjoyment of it.

(*And that's what I've done with my life.*)

Today he is the one who comes running up the staircase and the sound of his malevolent footsteps perpetuates the terror and death he had intended to fight. He has brought into the world all that he intended to banish from it. None of the goals he once pursued can absolve him of this. It is impossible to understand what has happened. He has lost everything. His only contact with mathematics comes down to the sordid statistical calculations which pepper his confidential reports. He has spoiled everything that was offered to him, exhausted God's mercy and his soul lies somewhere, very far behind him.

*

Robert Clément looks terrible. He cannot have been able to get a wink of sleep all night. His eyes are sunken and gleaming. A little acne spot has appeared at the corner of his mouth, just under his moustache. His breathing is very heavy. Capitaine Degorce is surprised that just one night should have put him in such a state. He knows he will talk soon. He squats beside him.

"You see, the nights are difficult," he says and his tone is exactly the same as the previous day, serene and courteous, as if nothing had happened. "Suppose we put an end to all this?"

"I've nothing to say to you," Clément replies. "How many times do I have to tell you?"

"I've no idea!" says Capitaine Degorce in surprise. "You can tell me as often as you like! I know it's not true, that's the only thing that matters."

He turns to Moreau and Febvay. "Our friend doesn't look too good, does he? It's really stupid to be as stubborn as this, don't you agree?"

"Agreed, mon capitaine, it's bloody stupid."

The *harkis* agree in a similar vein.

"Do you hear, Monsieur Clément? Your attitude produces

142

unanimity it seems. Don't you understand that you're going to get tired before we do?"

Clément looks down for a moment before signalling to Capitaine Degorce, who leans towards him. Clément spits in his face again.

"I shan't get tired. Not as long as I can spit in the face of a fascist bastard like you."

Capitaine Degorce was mistaken. What he took for weariness and despair was simply hatred, a terrible hatred further nourished by a night of solitude and sleeplessness. He wipes his face with a handkerchief and goes to fetch a glass of water. His heart is beating fast. The word "fascist" is intolerable. He thinks again of Tahar, he pictures his cold corpse, the terrible rictus from the hanging, while Clément is alive and staring at him arrogantly, Clément, a usurper of sufferings that are not his own, who imagines his treason makes him a hero. Clément's mind is a monolith, an impregnable citadel protected by walls of certainty. He will not talk.

(*Son of a bitch.*)

The sound of the glass breaking makes the soldiers start. Capitaine Degorce has flung it against the wall without saying a word and moves towards Clément, seizing him by the collar before giving him a headbutt. The capitaine unties him from his chair and throws him across the table, he bangs his head against the solid wood several times, Clément begins groaning, blood flows from his broken nose, the capitaine rips the buttons off his trousers and begins to slide them down his legs. Clément tries to defend himself, he lashes out violently, heaving his back off the table, but the capitaine thrusts his elbow into his stomach, leaning on it with all his weight, and Clément begins to vomit. A *harki* holds his shoulders down on the table while Capitaine Degorce finishes removing his trousers and rips his underpants. Then he puts his hands under Clément's legs and bends his legs back onto his chest in the position of a baby being changed.

"Febvay, your knife. Hold his legs."

With one hand Capitaine Degorce grabs Clément's genitals and presses them back onto his belly. He holds the ice cold point of the knife against his anus. Clément utters a brief piercing cry. The capitaine pushes the blade in half a centimetre until a thin trickle of warm blood runs down between his white buttocks. Clément howls.

"There's nothing wrong with you, do you understand?" the capitaine says in a hoarse, rasping voice. "There's nothing wrong with you, you filthy swine. You just need to relax because if you don't, you'll do yourself an injury. Can you relax, do you think? Relax!"

Somewhere invisible dykes have been swept away by the fury of a fierce torrent, welling up from a bottomless abyss, the torrent is in spate, nothing can stop it, it sweeps away the grief, the tormenting doubts, and Capitaine Degorce surrenders himself to the delights of the power racing through him and setting him free, a veil has fallen from his eyes, he feels his heart beating fit to burst in every part of his awakened body, at the corners of his mouth, in his belly, in his fingertips, in the palm of the hand holding the quivering dagger, and he leans over Clément to inhale the sweet, heady smell of his fear. The hatred has vanished. At one blow Capitaine Degorce has robbed him of the hatred that animated him and caused him to hold up and now he spits back in Clément's face and with unspeakable pleasure watches him caving in.

"Relax," he whispers softly. "Relax."

Clément tries to control his breathing and the involuntary contractions of his muscles. He closes his eyes with a groan. His limbs shake.

Clément is still. Tears flow from his eyelids and he sniffs noisily.

"I don't know what state you'll be in by the end of this interrogation. That depends on you. I'm going to ask you some questions. Not many. If you don't answer, or if you give me an answer I don't like, I shall push the knife in a little further, do you understand? I shall push it in like this."

He thrusts the blade in an extra half-centimetre. Clément opens his eyes wildly and begins emitting piercing yells, his body contracts and he howls still louder. The *harki* leans on his shoulders and Febvay is almost stretched out across his legs.

"There, there, there . . ."

A gentle lullaby. Febvay has his eyes half closed. The pink tip of his tongue shows between his lips.

"I want you to understand that I'm no longer joking," says Capitaine Degorce when Clément has again gained control of himself. "Begin now."

Clément gives names. Two Algerians and two French communist militants, a garage mechanic and a teacher. Capitaine Degorce removes the dagger and holds it close to Clément's eyes.

"A centimetre, you see, barely a centimetre. You're not worth anything, really, are you? Nothing at all. You'd have done better to listen to me. It's so easy to set things to rights, you see."

He turns to Moreau.

"Go and find those men, Moreau. And make them talk to me. The Frenchmen as well as the others. More than the others, the swine. Understood? I don't care about the publicity. And don't forget to let them know who gave us their names."

Clément sobs. Capitaine Degorce observes him with disgust. And he recognizes the same disgust in Febvay's eyes and Moreau's and those of the *harkis*, as well as admiration, the shifty gleam of connivance. There is saliva on the table and blood. Clément has turned on his side, his head cradled in his arms. His shrivelled penis dangles idiotically towards the table beneath the tuft of pubic hair. His thin legs, speckled with russet hairs, tremble convulsively. His feet are very white and delicate, the feet of a girl, but the nails are too long, irregular, and one of his little toes is dark, almost black. The storm has passed. All that remains is the ruins of a wasted landscape, and, amid the ruins, Clément's body, this mysterious and repellent victim's body. Capitaine Degorce feels nauseous.

"Show them how to live, Moreau," he nonetheless remarks.

*

He has completed the organization chart, spoken on the telephone to the colonel and acquiesced respectfully in all his lies. All desire for revolt has left him. He is resigned to his infamy and he only wants one thing now: to be finished as quickly as possible with the mission that keeps him here. He has no idea what awaits him after this, but it is all a matter of indifference. He paces along the corridors, goes from one interrogation room to another, his eyes hardly settle on the faces of the Arabs, and those of the garage mechanic and the teacher, their expressions do not count, they mean nothing. These faces are theatrical masks and pain will cause them to shatter in pieces. A long lament arises somewhere in the building.

"*Tahar, ia Tahar!*"

Another voice responds: "*Tahar, ia Tahar! Allah irahmek!*"

Another voice calls out in turn: "*Allah irham ech-chuhada!*"

"What are they saying?" Capitaine Degorce asks.

"They know about Hadj Nacer," replies a *harki*. "They're saying that his soul is with God."

"How do they know?"

Moreau spreads his hands in a helpless gesture.

"Make them be quiet," orders Capitaine Degorce. "I don't want to hear them anymore."

He steps aside to smoke a cigarette. First there is a clatter of doors opening, one after the other, then shouting and finally silence. There is no end to the afternoon. The wind drives a winter sky before it, laden with rain. The sun dries the wet pavements. And it is the same monotony, the same emptiness. The essential truth has been revealed and nothing new will happen. On all fours in his office he retrieves the torn fragments of the letter from Jeanne-Marie out of the depths of the wastepaper basket. Patiently he tries to piece it together and when he has finished dusk has fallen. He does not know if this was only a way of passing the time or if he is incapable of resigning himself to solitude. The words that bring him pain help him to feel alive.

"My child, my beloved, André, no news today. I don't feel like talking to you about the children and the petty aspects of our life far away from you. It's night and you're so very far away. If I didn't know you I could believe that you no longer love us. Your letters are so short and so cold. But I know you, I know the purity of your soul, your honesty, and I cannot believe it. So I know you are suffering and don't want to talk about it."

(*But I no longer have a soul.*)

A tear in the paper makes the start of the next sentence illegible.

"... for everything that torments you. And so I shall wait for the time it takes and you will share your pain with me. I'm almost an old woman, but there's nothing I could not hear from you, that's the advantage of being married to an older woman! If you want to continue carrying a burden that is too heavy for you all on your own, André, then do so if you must, but don't forget that I'm here to carry my share of it and that you can speak to me whenever you want to. Distance makes everything more difficult, my child, but I'm certain that when you're close to me it will be easy for you to talk and I know, too, that you'll need to do so. In the meantime please at least tell me I'm not mistaken. I know I'm not mistaken, but I should like you to write and tell me this, without any specifics, if you like, but write and tell me, for I'm going through some difficult nights. Oh, I'm not reproaching you, André, I'm asking you a favour. And I'll go on talking to you about peaches and the marvellous spring we're having here, I'll give you all the details, the scent of the *maquis*, now the flowers are out, the children's games, their whims, when they're being naughty little things, and their sweetness and our family outings. I shall go on so you may know we're all here, and there's a place for you forever in our hearts where nothing has changed. I shall ask nothing more of you and I'll expect you will be ready to . . ."

"Mon capitaine, you must come at once."

*

Robert Clément is lying on his side on the floor of his cell, the lower part of his naked body wrapped in a military blanket. His arms are pressed against his chest, black with dried blood. There is blood on the tiled floor, all around him a vast pool spreading towards the walls and disappearing beneath the straw mattress. One foot sticks out from the blanket and its milky whiteness is like a patch of light in the darkness. Adjudant-chef Moreau soaks a sponge in a bucket of water and gently wipes Clément's arms, on which the furrows of deep, jagged cuts appear where the pallid skin is torn. Capitaine Degorce crouches beside Moreau and takes the sponge from him. He squeezes it to expel all the blood and rinses it until the water that trickles out of it is perfectly clear and pure. He turns Clément onto his back and delicately raises his head, which sticks to the floor because of the blood. He runs the sponge over the face, the hair, the open eyes that are reluctant to close. The acne spot is still there, beneath the ridiculous moustache. His tightly closed lips are almost blue.

"How did he do that?" asks Capitaine Degorce.

"I've no idea, mon capitaine," Moreau says. "I don't understand."

Close to the body, stuck fast in the blood, a soldier finds a curved piece of plastic, about ten centimetres long and crudely sharpened, which he hands to Capitaine Degorce. Clément must have spent a long time rubbing it against the walls of his cell. In one sense his resolution had held firm. It had just been totally concentrated on a different objective.

"Where did he find that? What is it?"

"I've no idea, mon capitaine," repeats Moreau.

"It looks like a bit of the seat from the shithouse, mon capitaine," observes a soldier. "Do you want me to check?"

The capitaine silently shakes his head.

"I don't know when we screwed up, mon capitaine," says Moreau in a stricken voice.

"I don't hold it against you, Moreau," says the capitaine. "We've all screwed up, as you say, and I don't think it's important to know when."

Capitaine Degorce makes another vain attempt to close Clément's eyes. He straightens up slowly. He studies his bloodied shoes which make a sucking noise as he raises them from the floor.

"Clean the cell for me," he says. "And finish washing the boy."

He looks at Clément again, the milky whiteness of his skin, his open eyes that no longer see anything.

"Come with me, Moreau."

In his office he places a file on top of the torn-up letter from Jeanne-Marie.

"Robert Clément was released this morning after being questioned," he says to Moreau, carefully articulating each word. "Tonight you will take his body and make it disappear, I don't want to know how. I just want to be certain it will never be found. Understood?"

"Yes, mon capitaine," Moreau agrees. "But you know," he says after a while. "No-one will ever believe he was released and vanished like that into thin air."

The capitaine shrugs.

"What does it matter, Moreau, what people believe or not? What does it matter?"

Capitaine Degorce lowers his head and massages his brow with his fingertips. "And now leave me alone, please."

*

Within every man the memory of all humanity is perpetuated. And as for the immensity of all that there is to know, each one of us knows it already. That is why there will be no forgiveness. Capitaine Degorce has gone to find the Bible in his bedroom. He strokes its worn cover. There is a terrible sentence somewhere in the Gospel of St John that he needs to read and he reads: "But Jesus did not commit himself unto them because he knew all men, and needed not that any should testify of man: for he knew what was in man." He takes a sheet of paper and stares at the blank page without writing anything.

(*A voice has returned to me, Jeanne-Marie, but what can I do with it? For a long time I've been a prey to lies. I know what there is in man, I've seen it so many times and have never spoken of it. That's how I have gone on living. All I ever wrote to the families of all my comrades who died at my side in the prison camp was a web of lies. I spoke of courage, of sacrifice, of pride. I should have told them: your husband died because of me, your brother died because of me, or your son. I couldn't save them. I didn't want to. They died because they saw men accepting to live like insects, men like me. They died because they couldn't bring themselves to do this and because, when they looked at us, myself and my fellow men, they asked themselves, what's the point of living? Where we were, Jeanne-Marie, no-one could ask such a question and survive. Of course, there's someone who has a place in your loving heart, Jeanne-Marie, and also the hearts of the children, but it is not me. As for me I have no dwelling, not even in hell. As they reach out to you my arms ought to disintegrate into ashes. The pages of the holy Book ought to burn my eyes. If you could see what I am you would shield your face and Claudie would turn away from me in horror. That's how it is. Something wells up in man, something hideous, which is not human, and yet it is the essence of man, his profound truth. All the rest is merely lies. Spring is a lie, Jeanne-Marie, the sky is not blue and this very day I have killed a child and killed my brother. Undeserved love burdens us with a deadly weight. How could I tell you these things? A voice has returned to me for silence and for the night. A voice has returned to me for the dead who can no longer hear it.)*

"Mon capitaine, Andreani's men are here."

"Tell Moreau to take charge of handing over the prisoners. I'm busy. Give him the list."

Through the window he looks at the crescent of the moon, shining in a sky filled with stars. He feels as if he were performing an ageless ritual. In Jerusalem the storm of the crucifixion has passed and on the terrace of his palace the Procurator of Judaea raises his eyes clouded with longing towards the same moon. The heavy stone of the tomb has closed on the bodies of the execution victims and the silence of the night no longer makes them afraid.

(*How many faces does He have, Jeanne-Marie? Does He take pleasure in not being recognized so that we should go astray and turn away from Him while believing we are seeking Him? Is He evil? Does He rejoice to see us fall? Is it thus that He repays us for our weakness and our love? His body is ugly. No majesty emanates from it. He does not shine. His wounds are appalling and do not inspire compassion. He looks like a criminal broken by justice. No-one weeps over Him. Those who cannot hold back their tears on seeing Him are saved, but no-one weeps. You can see, I am not weeping. Implacable logic strengthens my mind and logic is useless to me, it turns inside out like a glove and all the countless reasons that caused me to accept His being tortured and to raise my hand against Him are as insubstantial as mist. And I raised my hand against Him, Jeanne-Marie, several times, and I did not recognize Him, power and logic armed my hand, gave it its strength, but this hand has fallen back, powerless and dead and I cannot now cause it never to have been raised. But He, Jeanne-Marie, He who can do everything. Could not He cause it never to have been raised? Could not He cause me to have repudiated my mind's logic and not Him? For now I have learned and I know. If it were given to me to encounter Him again I should recognize Him, whatever His face were like, I should recognize Him and I should know what to do. For I have also learned that evil is not the opposite of good: the frontiers between good and evil are confused, they blend into one another and become impossible to tell apart in the bleak grey light that covers everything and that is what evil is. And I have learned that the mind's desiccated logic can achieve nothing without the help*

153

*of the soul, it can only stray endlessly in the grey fog, lost between good and evil,
and I, Jeanne-Marie, have left my soul somewhere behind me, I can remember
neither where nor when. And what would be the point of my knowing if He
does not allow me to retrace my steps? And what is there for me to do other
than continue pressing on along the road that leads me ever further from Him
and you? I should like Him to take me back to the dawn of that day that is
erased from my memory, one that only He knows. The truth is that if anger
could still mean something to me I should be so angry with Him. Why did He
let me squander all the love I carried within me? Why did He let me make
myself unworthy of you? But He does not even grant me the grace of His anger,
Jeanne-Marie, I'm a whimpering animal, so cold I no longer even feel the pain
that makes me whimper, and although I know that I lost the right to pray a
long time ago, I pray all the same. All I wish is that He would let me return, if
only for a moment, to where I left my soul.)*

But everything fades away so quickly, Tahar's face, smiling
beneath the soft breeze that stirs the black curls of his hair, at
Taghit or Timimoun, and the echoes of Claudie's laughter on the
beach at Piana. Capitaine André Degorce goes back to sit at his
desk. He writes a single long sentence, an illegible scribble, into
which he puts all his love.

Oh no, mon capitaine, I shall not forget you and nor will you be able to forget me, I know that, for I have a very clear memory of reading somewhere that we must forever share the fate of those who have loved us, and the love I bore you is perhaps more pure and true than the love you were surrounded with by your parents, your wife and your children and all those who believed they loved you. Your contempt does not matter any more than mine, mon capitaine, it is powerless against the force of this love I have never managed to eradicate from my heart, for it has been rooted there like a weed, full of vitality, and I know now that nothing will eradicate it. You cannot imagine how much easier it would be for me simply to be your enemy, rather than submitting to the tyranny of the love that binds me to you. I understand that you may want no part in it, that it may fill you with horror, but remember that it was not my choice either, and if you are still capable of being honest you must admit that, apart from me, no-one has loved the man you really are, for, in truth, no-one apart from me has known you. You are well aware of this, neither your wife, nor the boy you have brought up, nor the daughter you so inconsiderately begot know you and I am certain you must often have wondered what would survive of their love, could they but glimpse, if only for a second, the man you really are, the one you have striven to conceal from them for all these years, while constantly dreading that they would nevertheless discover him, and I would swear, mon capitaine, that you have chosen to live in fear and silence rather than risk confronting the fragility of their love. But I know you, I know what an incredible coward you are, I know the taste of the resentments that burn your mouth, and your erring ways, your lies, I know the immensity of your weakness, your unquenchable thirst for punishment, I know your tormented conscience because I am your brother, remember we were sired by the same battle, under the monsoon rains, and I have never ceased to love you like a brother. Oh, I know your secret dreams, mon capitaine, I know them so well that on some nights I feel as if you are dreaming within me, or else it is me slipping in beside you in the dream in which we have been transported very far away from the pitiless country of my birth, that country which is no longer mine and has never been yours, and the two of us are walking along a desert road between Taghit and Béchar, by the light of a very yellow crescent moon, which hangs like a street lamp in a sky without stars, we are walking amid objects half covered in sand, scattered over the ground as far as the eye can see, court shoes with broken heels, torn dresses whose colours have been erased by the desert wind that has stripped out all the embroidery with golden threads, a collapsed *darbouka* drum, an *oud* with no strings, blackened clusters of jewels, little boxes of henna and kohl, satin trousers and fragments of china, good luck charms, a whole trousseau that has slowly petrified in my memory since the one who assembled it has decayed into dust, an eternity ago, mon capitaine, and now these bone-dry remains are not even stirred by the wind that blows so strongly. You look about you, but none of the ones you seek are there, no little girl playing in the sand, no little boy, your wife is not waiting for you anywhere and the man you have been hoping all your life to see again will not come back to you and you try to call out his name in the darkness, but you have no voice and no-one can hear you. There is only me, mon capitaine, and very close to us, at the foot of a dune, a little dromedary crying out for its mother over and over again, stretching out its neck beneath the moon, but it cannot see us for a compassionate hand has blinded it, so that our wolf eyes, gleaming in the darkness, should never terrify anyone again. You are trying to escape from me, mon capitaine, but the undying power of my love shackles me to you and you cannot contrive to do so, all your futile running has never got you anywhere, and however breathlessly you run, I am still there, every tattered dress, the dromedary and the *darbouka*, each blade of grass, each fragment of coral and silver is like one of the infinite centres of the unimaginable circle round whose circumference you persist in running for no reason, mon capitaine, since however long you went on running for, you will never reach Taghit, you will never know if someone is waiting for you in the cool of the palm grove, at the foot of the earth walls, to speak to you at last the words I did not allow him to utter in the darkness of a cellar during a night in spring, an eternity ago, and when you have understood this, you fall to your knees in the dust of the long desert road and you look up at the moon imploringly. In this dream, which is also your own, mon capitaine, the time has come when I go up to you to clasp you close to my heart like a brother. You do not push me away, you let yourself come to me, shaking with silent sobs, and I am so happy, mon capitaine, because I have understood that our dream will never set us free. We shall not leave one another. And the time has come when I lean gently towards you to whisper in your ear that we have arrived in hell, mon capitaine – and that your prayers have been answered.

Jérôme Ferrari

THE SERMON
ON THE FALL OF ROME

Translated from the French by Geoffrey Strachan

Winner of the 2012 Prix Goncourt

Available Autumn 2014

MACLEHOSE PRESS

www.maclehosepress.com
Subscribe to our quarterly newsletter